# Spirit Of Country

# Songwriter Series

# Book IV

## Joe Tallarigo

Joe Tallarigo

# Spirit Of Country

# Songwriter Series

# Book IV

Copyright © 2026

Written and designed by Joe Tallarigo

The pictures in this book are from my collection and Pixabay.

Some of these songs are based on real people, places, and events, and others are pure fiction from the author's imagination.

Published by Twin Hills Publishing LLC

ISBN: 978-1-7329930-6-8

# A Word From The Author

This book started in 2019 as I was driving through Lexington, Kentucky, following the comic con. A sense of tranquility came over me as I looked at the rolling green hills and horse meadows.

This book is the fourth installment in my Songwriters series, capturing my love of Country Music, enjoying life, Christmas, and just having good times.

This book is inspired by Kenny Chesney, Jimmy Buffett, George Strait, Tim McGraw, Alan Jackson, and every other 1990s country music singer.

This book is dedicated to my Aunt Sue and Uncle Dave, who made New Orleans their second home. Also to my friends Robin and Joani Lacy, who celebrated New Orleans and Zydeco Music with their band Robin Lacy and DeZydeco for thirty years.

This book is also dedicated to America, which will be celebrating its 250th birthday on July 4th, 2026.

To Lisa: Thanks for inspiring some of these poems and chasing your dreams!

You will notice at the end of every poem, the year I wrote it, along with my age. This is done to show when I wrote it, and you can follow the growth of my songwriting.
These songs were written from 2003 to 2026.

I hope you enjoy these poems, find the good in life, and that you pursue your dreams no matter how lofty or hard they may be. Life is about enjoying the moments that bring us love, laughter, and hope.

# Chapter One

# Spirit Of Country

# Spirit of Country

Country Radio plays it
Twenty-four seven
It's a secret ingredient
In Southern cooking
It's heard in the cry
Of a steel guitar
Girl Scouts sell it
In every box of cookies
Boys catch it
When they go fishing

It stretches from
Coast to Coast

Preachers preach it
During Sunday sermons
Politicians promote it
On their campaign trails
Teachers teach it
In their classrooms
It's found in the grounds
Of blood-soaked battlefields
It soars high in the sky
Standing in every town square

Its Colors are
Red, white, and blue

Joe Tallarigo

It's grown
In the American Heartland
It's felt in the wind
Blowing through Georgia Pines
It flows through
The blue-collar workers
Police and American Soldiers
Proudly wear it on duty
It's built in
Every American factory

The Great American Novels
Are inspired by it

It's mixed
Into strawberry wine
It's dreamed about
On every ballfield
It's carried on the box cars
Rolling down the tracks
It stays in our prayers
Every single night

You can feel it most
On Independence Day
During
The fireworks show.

**May 21, 2019**
**34 years old**

# Small Town Country Music Video

The morning sun debuts
Over that rustic water tower
Shining brightly on the crops below
A farmer
Fires up his tractor
Easing into his day
Cutting twenty acres
Before he's baling hay

It's the start of a
Small town Country Music video
Another long day
Of hard work
On his family farm
In the heat of a July sun
His wife brings him
A cold glass of lemonade
A turkey sandwich on rye
Bows his head, thankful
He's living the good life

He
drives into town
Smiling
Seeing his
1992 question

Caroline,
Will you
Go to prom with me
Painted in
Bright neon green
On the
Rustic water tower

Joe Tallarigo

It's the middle of a
Small town Country Music video
Running his weekly errands
Picking up parts for his tractor
Buying
Ham, corn, rolls, apple pie
For his
Weekly Saturday night dinner
With his in-laws

As the
Hot July sun sets
He and his wife, Caroline
Are rocking out
To a local country band
At their county fair

It's the end of a
Small town Country Music video
Pan the crowd as they
Get lost in the  music
Show the happy couple
Eating cotton candy
Capture the Ferris Wheel
Glowing bright
Record the
Sound of the Skee-ball
Going up the ramp

This is the good life
In a small town
In a
Small town Country Music video.

**\*\*May 26, 2019\*\***
**\*34 years old\*\***

# Horse Country

Blue skies reign over
Wide-open green pastures
Where the dawn rolls in
Gentle and slow
Miles of worn wooden fences
Mark paths where
The young cattle grow
Red barns stand
With the stories of seasons
Holding bales of
Last Summer's golden hay

Every kid has
Their own horse
Growing closer
With every passing ride
Each evening
They meet at the stables
Letting patience and courage
Be their guides
As they gallop through
Wide-open green pastures

There are
Rolling green hills
Made for climbing
Dusty old trails
Made for exploring
The stars
Are free to shine
With
No-one wishing for
Big city lights and dreams

Joe Tallarigo

Fresh laundry sways
On outside lines
Dogs tear through
Mud patches and grass
Holly's ice cream shop
Piles high the richest
Cookies and Cream sundaes

Joe's Gas Station
Once sold a winning
Thousand-dollar scratch off
With the winner
Throwing a huge
Town-wide party

Couples mingle
Sip a few drinks
Before they play
Golf all afternoon
At the
Green Briar Country Club

Give me the freedom
Amongst the
One-lane country roads
Where time moves slowly
Horses gallop fast
Feeling God's presence
In the
Wide-open green pastures
Here in
Horse Country.

**\*\*May 20, 2019\*\***
**\*\*34 years old\*\***

# Horse Country

Joe Tallarigo

# Kids And Their Dogs

Kids and their dogs
Chasing each other around their yard
Playing fetch with a slobbery ball
Digging holes, then burying
Their favorite toys and bones
In mama's garden

Kids and their dogs
Taking over the living room
Stretching out on the couch
Leaving space for nobody else
As they watch
Their favorite shows
All afternoon long

Kids feed their dogs
Table scraps
All sneaking treats
When their parents
Aren't around
All blue
When it rains
Wanting to be outside
Splashing in
the mud and puddles

Kids and their dogs
Make up for rainy days
Running free and wild
On wooded trails
Getting
Soaked and muddy
In the
Shallow streams

Kids and their dogs
Are adorable
As they crash
On the living room floor
Curling up together
Wiped out
After their long day
Playing in the fresh air
Don't you dare
Try to wake them
Or
They'll growl at you

Kids and their dogs
Will drive you crazy
When
They're
Cooped up inside
Wrestling and fighting
But once outside
They'll make you smile
As they
Play fetch with a slobbery ball

Kids and their dogs
Steal your heart
As they
Beg for treats
Then
Cuddle on the couch
To watch
Their favorite shows
All afternoon long.

**\*\*July 5, 2021\*\***
**\*\*36 years old\*\***

Joe Tallarigo

# To The Land, Man

She has her
Princess sleeping bag
Pink fishing pole in tow
Clothes piled in her bags
She has her
Sunglasses on
Flashlight in hand
She has a plan
For a weekend getaway

She's
Running around the house
Telling her
Mom, Dad, and Brother
Let's go to the land, man
Come on, let's go
I'm ready, why aren't you
Pack up the van
Get to land, man

Being
Cooped up all winter
Isn't ideal
For an outdoor girl
Who's only
Four years old

She's ready
To go fishing
Driving her princess jeep
On the back roads
Visiting
The cows and chickens
Living out a young
Country girl's dream

She says
Come on, let's go
I'm ready, why aren't you
Pack up the van
Get to the land, man

There are
No chores to do
You can make s'mores
In a fire pit
While counting
A million stars

There's also
Fresh country air
Every kind of wildlife
No calls to be made
It's the perfect
Weekend getaway

She's
Running around the house
Telling her
Mom, Dad, and Brother
Pack up the van, man
Let's go to the land, man
Start the van, man
Let's get on the road, man
Must get to the land, man.

**\*\*January 23, 2012\*\***
**\*\*27 years old\*\***

# To The Land, Man

# Mama's Train

My sister and I
Had to be in bed
By nine
Every night
I count the box cars
Rolling on by
To help me fall asleep

Always
Telling my mama
Before
Going up the stairs
One day
I'm going to
Ride those rails

The lonesome whistle
Plays like a song
Dreaming
What It'll be like
To ride in the pale moonlight
Across bridges, past cornfields
Along mountainsides
Seeing all of America
Through my young eyes

I'd
Call my mama
Telling her
I'm having a good time
Riding the rails
In the pale moonlight
Tell my sister
I said hi

Joe Tallarigo

Mama
Reads us stories
About
Fairies and pirates
My sister's favorites are
Peter Pan, Treasure Island

Though
I'd rather hear about
Casey Jones
He was a rolling stone
Engineering his train
Down the rails

I'd
Ride with him from
Southern Alabama
To Northern Alaska
Traveling on the trestles
In the pale moonlight
Across bridges, past cornfields
Along the mountainsides
Seeing all of America
Through my young eyes

I'd
Call up my mama
Telling her
I'm having a good time
Riding the rails
In the pale moonlight
Tell my sister
I said hi.

**April 26, 2010**
**25 years old**

# Mama's Train

Joe Tallarigo

# A Good Sunday

A good Sunday
Is waking up early
Eating
Pancakes, sausages, bacon
With your family

Getting dressed
In your Sunday best
Following along in the bible
As the Preacher
Gives his sermon
Praying solemnly for
Family, friends, and the sick
Then, after the final Amen
Pulling into Denny's
To have a good lunch

A good sundae
Has three scoops
Of ice cream
Topped with
Whipped cream, hot fudge,
Sprinkles and cherries

Picking out a good movie
Eating it slowly
Not devouring it in the
First ten minutes
Avoiding a brain freeze
Enjoying
The sweet, savory taste
A well-deserved treat
To end
The work week

A good sun day
Is enjoying
A cool breeze
Blowing through the trees
A picnic basket full of
Your favorite foods
Holding your lover's hand
Strolling in the sand
Rubbing sunscreen
On her skin
For she wants
A good tan

As you
Swim in the water
You wave to her
As she looks up
From her favorite book
She gives you
A bright smile

Both feeling
Like you
Won the lottery
Watching the sunset
On this
Beautiful sun day.

**\*\*June 3, 2019\*\***
**\*\*34 years old\*\***

Joe Tallarigo

# Gibbs And His Cows

He's jumping on my lap
Looking to the left
Looking to the right
A big ol' smile on his face
He's in his happy place
Eyes wide open
Searching every fence line
For his cow friends

He's a
Cow-loving canine
Farm living, day-dreaming
Friend of mine
His heart races when we
Cross the
Indiana state line
Knowing we're
Going down the backroads
That leads to
His favorite farms
To visit his cow friends

He spots a herd
Hanging out
Against the fence line
He whimpers
Jumps to the backseat
Tail wagging
Looks out the window
His wide eyes
Dart back and forth
Can't believe his luck
Seeing how many
Cows there are

He's a
Cow-loving canine
Farm living, day-dreaming
Friend of mine
His heart races when we
Cross the
Indiana state line
Knowing we're
Going down the backroads
That leads to his favorite farms
To visit his cow friends

He wants to get out
Run up to the fence
Sneak his way in
To give all the cows
A sloppy wet kiss
Run around with them
Having
The best day of
His young canine life

He's a
Cow-loving canine
Farm living, day-dreaming
Friend of mine
His heart races when we
Cross the
Indiana state line
Knowing we're
Going down the backroads
That leads to his favorite farms
To visit his cow friends.

**December 10, 2025**
**40 years old**

Joe Tallarigo

# Gibbs And His Cows

# Here For The Summer
## (Part One)

Her tan lines glowing
As she chases fireflies
I can't help staring
She spins around, smiles
Says, "Come follow me,"
She kicks off her shoes
Disappears into the meadow

As
I follow
To my surprise
She pounces
Pins me down
Laughing
As we hit the ground

Says
"Look here, city boy"
You're new to this
One-red-light town
This country girl
Will be happy
To show you around,"

Staring
Into her
Sappy brown eyes
All I can mutter is
"What a bummer
I'm only
Here for the Summer
Helping my uncle
Fix up his farm,"

Joe Tallarigo

She says
"That's enough time for
Tasting my famous lemonade
Pushing each other
On my tire swing
Going fishing
Teaching you how to make
Strawberry jam
Showing you my collection
Of every deer bone
I find in these fields"

She gets off me
Dusts herself off
Helps me up
Kisses me on the cheek
My temperature rising
As she says

"Get a lot of sleep
You'll need
All your strength
Hanging out with me,"

As I
Drift off to sleep
Her words
Makes my heart flutter
Never met a girl
Like her before
Making me wish
This Summer lingers.

**May 21, 2019**
**34 years old**

# Here For The Summer
## (Part 2)

I almost
Fall off the ladder
As she strolls up
To my uncle's gate
In her Braves jersey
Looking like fate
She grins and asks
"Are you free?"

I reply
"Girl, you're in luck
My uncle's away
Running errands all day,"

She grabs my hand
Pulls me down
An old dirt path
Leading to a pond
She jumps right in
Says
"Don't be shy,
Come join me,"
Then
Playfully splashes me

We shake off the pond
Fireflies dancing all around
Barefoot in the meadow
Moonlight casting shadows
I catch her eyes
The world fades
We fall in the grass
Rolling
Chasing sparks between us

Joe Tallarigo

I've heard
The South was hot
Never imagining
I'd be enjoying
This Summer heat
With a
Georgia peach
Wishing
I could stay longer
Past this Summer

I'm Sure
Going to miss
Her Southern accent
Her playfulness
She'll always have
A piece of my heart

Maybe next year
I'll meet her
Under the pines
As the
Madison stars shine
Picking up
Where we left off

Staying much longer
Than
This short Summer.

**May 21, 2019**
**34 years old**

# Cornfields At Midnight

Oh Girl
I'd like to take you
To a secret place
Where
Only I go
Three A.M. secrets
Gets lost
As the morning sun
Breaks through the dawn

Midnight in a cornfield
Wind whispers low
Every breath
Makes my heart glow
Fireflies blink
Like they're
In on our fun
Two young lovers
Having
One magical moment
Deep in a cornfield
At midnight

The
Scarecrows watching
But he won't tell
Hearts racing fast
Holding each other
Stealing sweet kisses
Between the rows
Out in the dark
Just you and me
Laughing and flirting
Wild and free

Joe Tallarigo

Midnight in a cornfield
Wind whispers low
Every breath
Makes my heart glow
Fireflies blink
Like they're
In on our fun
Two young lovers
Having
One magical moment
Deep in a cornfield
At midnight

Crickets and frogs
Play our favorite tune
We're
Dancing in the shadows
Under the Harvest Moon
You pull me near
Whispering things
I only want to hear

Midnight in a cornfield
Wind whispers low
Every breath
Makes my heart glow
Fireflies blink
Like they're
In on our fun
Two young lovers
Having
One magical moment
Deep in a cornfield
At midnight.

**December 12, 2025**
**41 years old**

# Hillbilly Dance Party

Fire up the lanterns
String those lights
High in the loft
Don't need any DJ
To spin our favorite songs
Chris and Jill brought their
Fiddle and Banjo
To entertain us
Just make sure
You have
Your best boots on

It's a
Hillbilly Dance Party
Kick the doors wide open
The barn will shake
Like never before
Stomping all night
On the wooden floor
Drinking punch
That packs a punch
Giving some a
Moonlit buzz

Cow-girls
In worn-out jeans
Spin me 'round
To this backwoods beat
Feel the country spirit
Rising in this Summer heat
If it gets to be too much
We can take a break
Get to know each other
On a hay bale seat

Joe Tallarigo

It's a
Hillbilly Dance Party
Kick the doors wide open
The barn will shake
Like never before
Stomping all night
On the wooden floor
Drinking punch
That packs a punch
Giving some a
Moonlit buzz

The music stops
As old-man Jenkins
Enters in his
Mud-covered overalls
Dust on his cowboy hat
His hands blistered
Says

"It's time I joined in
Been over twenty years
Since I took the time
To let loose
There's more to life
Than working
In the Summer suns,"

It's a
Hillbilly Dance Party
With
Good music and friends
Lasting 'til the cows come home.

**December 14, 2025**
**41 years old**

# Rustic Rocking Chair

There's a
Rustic rocking chair
Sitting proudly
On a rotted rotunda
Just outside of
Nebraska, Indiana
That still rocks
Every time a
Gentle wind blows

All the locals say
That's Mr. Roberts
Still rocking in that
Rustic rocking chair
Still enjoying
His country living
Watching the corn grow
Smiling every time
A gentle wind blows

He Should be
In Heaven
He's chosen to stay
In his favorite chair
Where he
Spent every night
Rocking his newborns
To sleep
Waving to his neighbors
Driving by on Sunday's
When there was a problem
He'd sit there all afternoon
'Til
He came up with a solution

Joe Tallarigo

There's a
Rustic rocking chair
Sitting proudly
On a rotted rotunda
Just outside of
Nebraska, Indiana
That still rocks
Every time a
Gentle wind blows

The town council
Can't bring themselves
To tearing down
That crumbling house
Evicting that
Rustic rocking chair
For Mr. Roberts
Was the
Towns first mayor
Left it in his will
His house and rocking chair
Would always remain
For he loved this town

Now
Some say
In the
Full moon light
It's a calming sight
Seeing Mr. Roberts
Rocking his children
To sleep
In that
Rustic rocking chair

**December 25, 2025**
**41 years old**

# John Deere, Dear John

My wife hinted at wanting
Something big and fancy
For her thirtieth birthday
So I bought her a
John Deere tractor
In return, she sent me a
Dear John letter

I'm missing my iced tea
That she would bring me
The chores are piling up
Weekly meals are a no-go
Can't find my lucky fishing poles
To go fishing at my favorite creek
Can't believe she left me
For buying her a
John Deere tractor

It's a shade of bright green
She would never wear
Has a lot of torque
To get the chores done faster
So I could
spend more time with her

I'm missing my iced tea
That she would bring me
The chores are piling up
Weekly meals are a no-go
Can't find my lucky fishing poles
To go fishing at my favorite creek
Can't believe she left me
For buying her a
John Deere tractor

Joe Tallarigo

Her favorite singers are
Jason Aldean, Kenny Chesney
Both
Sing songs about tractors
That was a major factor
Wanting to spend
Every evening with her
Riding on the back roads
On her
Big and fancy tractor

I still read her
Dear John letter
As I drive her
John Deere tractor
Wishing

I had
A glass of iced tea
Still can't find my fishing poles
To go fishing at my favorite creek
But
Thanks to the internet
I'm preparing weekly meals

If only I could find
A fool-proof plan
To bring her back to me

I guess
What she really wanted
Was a
Big fancy diamond ring.

**May 20, 2019**
**34 years old**

# Our GPS

The moon and stars
Were our guides
Through the night
We were in trouble
When dense clouds
Delayed our journey

We built
Canoes and ships
By sail and oars
We traveled the oceans
Relying on telescopes
To guide us
To our destinations
As we
Bought and traded
Our spices and timber

Traveling
To Oregon
We began
In the Great Plains
In our wagon trains
We passed by
Chimney Rock
Fort Laramie
Fort Hall
Boise to Whittman Mansion
Ending our treacherous
Five-month journey
Two thousand miles away
From where
We first began
To start our new life

Joe Tallarigo

Soon our directions
Was printed out on paper
Go past the Thompsons' house
Turn left at the pizza parlor
Continue past the stop sign
You'll come upon a
Five and dime
In a mile, turn right
You'll see a farm
That's where you'll buy
The eggs and tomatoes

Now we have
GPS
Installed in our cars
Installed on our phones
Telling us
The fastest way
How long
It'll take to get there
Rerouting us
When roads are blocked

There's
No more imagination
When traveling
No more magic
Of finding
Tourist traps
Hideaway restaurants
Off beaten-paths
Thanks to our
GPS.

**October 1, 2019**
**34 years old**

# Ode To Trains

Iron trestles still lay
Across this great land
Kids and adults
Still enjoy
Riding the trains
From
Coast to coast

There's something magical
Stepping onto the tracks
Staring down the line
Dreaming
What it would feel like
Jumping on a freight train
Playing hobo
For a few days
Seeing where I end up

I've been
To small towns
Where the trestles
Are only feet away
From people's houses
Making me wonder
How can they live like that

Do their pictures
Fall off the walls
As the trains roll by
Do they
Set their clocks
By the train schedules
Do they even notice
The trains at all

Joe Tallarigo

On
Dark lonely nights
I'm thankful
For the chance
Hearing a
Lonesome whistle moaning
And
The sound of boxcars
Rumbling down the line
Stirring
My rambling soul

So
I go down
To the tracks
Walk along them
As far as I can
Dreaming
What it would feel like
Jumping on a freight train
Playing hobo
For a few days
Seeing where I end up.

**\*\*July 12, 2012\*\***
**\*\*27 years old\*\***

# Stars and Pine Cones
## (Part One)

I
Cherish the nights
We would sit
On your front porch
Watching
All the stars
Dance in the night sky
You
Called them balloons
As we tried
To count them all

Then
You would get distracted
By the shining moon
Airplanes and their lights

I
Cherish the days
We would spend
In your front yard
Collecting
All the pine cones
We found on the ground
You would
Sort them from the
Smallest to the biggest

Then
You cared for them
As if they were
Your baby dolls

Joe Tallarigo

Oh
To be that young again
Seeing the world anew
Running barefoot
Through the tall grass
Painting the world
With different
Designs and hues
Watching every sunset
With no regrets
Never being too busy
For family and friends

Stars and pine cones
Painting, blowing bubbles
Keeping me young
Doing these things
With you

I know
One day
You'll be a teen
Looking back
On these days
And
You'll smile

Stars and pine cones.

**November 12, 2012**
**27 years old**

# Stars and Pine Cones
## (Part One)

# Chapter Two

# The Magic Of Christmas

(Christmas 1990)

# The Weeks Leading Up To Christmas

Store employees are busy
Painting their business windows
With winter and manger scenes
Stocking every shelf
With the hottest new toys
Displaying the ugly sweaters
To wear to your office party
Santa is sitting on his throne
Taking pictures with every child
Everything you need is here
To get you in the Christmas Spirit

The
Official Christmas Tree
Arrives in the town square
Soon it'll shine bright with
Stringed lights, ornaments, tinsel
It's that time again
For the official
Christmas Tree lighting
With Mayor Jones
Emceeing the ceremonies

Couples are ice skating
Families are attending
Local Christmas parades
Then putting up
Their Christmas decorations
Kids are excited for
Eating breakfast with Santa
While
Counting down the days
To the start of
Christmas Break

Joe Tallarigo

It's time to
Binge-watch
Your favorite
Christmas specials
Eating
Candy canes, Andes Mints
Buying and wrapping gifts
Baking every kind of cookie
Listening to your favorite carols

Sit down to write
Personal Christmas cards
Pray for snow
On Christmas Eve
So when
Family and friends arrive
It'll be an
Old-fashioned Christmas

The weeks
Leading up to Christmas
Are my favorite weeks
Of every passing year
So much to do
In so little time

Have to
Look at all the displays
Make figure-eights
Make snow angels
Drink hot chocolate
Feeling the Christmas Spirit
Like I did as a kid.

**July 21, 2021**
**36 years old**

# First Snow Of December

Jack Frost winds
Chill the playground swings
Gray sky smiling
Like it's up to something
Kids blowing their breaths
Pretending to be dragons
Some run-in place
To keep warm
Others begin to chant
Come on snow-day

It's 11:00 A.M.
Big snowflakes
Begin to take over
Turning the blacktop
Into Frosty's home
Teachers yelling
But we don't hear
Too busy trying to catch
The first snowflakes
On our tongues

First snow
Of December
Falling on us
Our gloves getting wet
Tossing snowballs
At our friends
Building our first snowman
Holding the girls' hands
Pretending we're
Walking in a winter wonderland
Teachers are scrambling
To get us back inside
Why don't they understand

Joe Tallarigo

The First snow of December
Is purely magical
Can build anything
Our heart desires
First sled ride
Down the biggest hill
Is always a thrill
Always hoping
For a snow day

It's 11:00 A.M.
Big snowflakes
Begin to take over
Turning the blacktop
Into Frosty's home
Teachers yelling
But we don't hear
Too busy trying to catch
The first snowflakes
On our tongues

First snow of December
Falling on us
Our gloves getting wet
Tossing snowballs
At our friends
Building our first snowman
Holding the girls' hands
Pretending we're
Walking in a winter wonderland
Teachers are scrambling
To get us back inside
Why don't they understand?

**December 17, 2025**
**41 years old**

# Breakfast With Santa

Snow on the ground
Icy chill in the air
Red and green sweaters
All around
All my family is here
Standing in line
To get enough seats
Smell of bacon and pancakes
Makes me joyfully shake
Knowing it's almost time

The other kids
Are buzzing louder
Then the old bell rings
Candy canes are being
Passed down the line
A sweet treat
To help pass the time
'Til the doors open
Being rushed on
By excited children

It's
Breakfast with Santa
Pancakes piled high
Syrup on our fingers
Wonder in our eyes
Joy in our hearts
My favorite start
To the Christmas season
Holiday cheer in the air
Magical feeling everywhere
Having
Breakfast with Santa

Joe Tallarigo

Cameras flashing bright
Sitting on this
Christmas legends knees
Dressed in his red and white
Kids rattling off
Their Christmas lists
Not thinking twice
If they've been
Naughty or nice

Our eyes glow
Listening to him
Telling familiar stories
Of
Rudolph the Red-Nosed Reindeer
The elves keeping busy
Throughout the year
Making all the toys
By their magical hands

It's
Breakfast with Santa
Pancakes piled high
Syrup on our fingers
Wonder in our eyes
Joy in our hearts
My favorite start
To the Christmas season
Holiday cheer in the air
Magical feeling everywhere
Having
Breakfast with Santa.

**December 18, 2025**
**41 years old**

# Magic Of Christmas

I still believe in
The magic of Christmas
The wonderful feelings
Of joy and awe
Just like when I was
A young child
Nothing in this world
Will ever change that
Not even getting older

I can still find
The magic of Christmas
In every holiday
Movie, cartoon, concerts
It's in the
Blinking Christmas lights
Stockings hanging by the fireplace
The faces of every child
Looking up at the night sky
On Christmas Eve

I can still feel
The magic of Christmas
Putting homemade ornaments
On the Christmas tree
Picking out the
Perfect collectible gift
Celebrating the birth
Of our
Lord and Savior
With
Family and friends
At Midnight Mass

Joe Tallarigo

There are times
It's hard to get into
The Christmas Spirit
When the Heat Miser
Turns up the temperatures
An early taste of Spring
With no
Jack Frost winds blowing
Snow on the ground
To build a snowman
Or go sled riding

That's the time
I reach deep in my soul
Recall the days of yore
Bringing back the
Magic of Christmas

The magic of Christmas
Still resides in
Getting pictures with Santa
Lighting up the Christmas tree
For the first time
Writing Christmas blessings
To family and friends
Decorating every room
With your childhood decorations
Drinking hot cocoa
Eating candy canes
Wearing matching pjs
Waking up together on Christmas
With many presents under the tree.

**November 21, 2022**
**37 years old**

# Meet Me Under The Mistletoe

Family and friends are here
Swapping family tales
Grandma is rocking out
On the piano
Imitating Brenda Lee
Bringing joy and cheer
As she performs

The kids are asking
Every three minutes
When will Santa be here
They want their presents now

All this
Celebrating is nice
But quite honestly, my dear
All I want is your
Warmth and charm
So, will you meet me
Under the mistletoe

Meet me under the mistletoe
Like you did all those years ago
When my ugly sweater
Caught your eye
Meet me under the mistletoe
I want to see the glow
Of the Christmas lights
In your soft brown eyes
Recreate the magic we felt
As our lips first met
Then
We'll sneak out
To play in the midnight snow

Joe Tallarigo

It's quiet here now
Everyone's gone home
The piano keys
Are getting a rest
The food and drinks
Are put away
The wooden blocks
Are stacked high
The train engine
Is back in the station

There's only
One more hour
Of this
Christmas Season
I believe
That's a good reason
To meet me under
The mistletoe

Meet me under the mistletoe
Like you did all those years ago
When my ugly sweater
Caught your eye
Meet me under the mistletoe
I want to see the glow
Of the Christmas lights
In your soft brown eyes
Recreate the magic we felt
As our lips first met
Then
We'll sneak out
To play in the midnight snow.

**November 16, 2015**
**30 years old**

54

# A Cincinnati Sports Fan Christmas Wish

It's 11:55 P.M.
Time to set out
Skyline cheese coney's
A case of Barq's Root Beer
A pint of Grater's Ice Cream
A box of Grippo's Chips
Autographs picture of
Joe Burrow
Elly De La Cruz

Time to amp up
My Christmas wish
Butter-up Santa
Convince him
He needs to
Use his Christmas magic
To bring multiple
Super Bowl Championships
World Series Championships
To all
Cincinnati sports fans

Wouldn't it be great
To finally celebrate
A Cincinnati Bengals
Super Bowl win
Bringing together all
Generations of fans
Finally erasing
All the
Heart-breaking history
Fans have endured
For
Over fifty-years

Joe Tallarigo

Santa, is it a deal
Skyline Cheese coney's
A case  of Barq's Root Beer
A pint of Grater's Ice Cream
a box of Grippo's chips
A Joe Burrow
Autograph picture
For multiple
Bengals Super Bowl Championships

I was in Kindergarten
Celebrating the
1990 Reds
World Series Sweep
Attended game three
Of the 2012 playoffs
Since then the
Postseasons have been
Heartbreaking
Many young fans
Need to celebrate
A Cincinnati Reds
World Series Championship

Santa, is it a deal
Skyline cheese coney's
A case of Barq's Root Beer
A pint of Grater's Ice Cream
A box of Grippo's chips
A Elly De La Cruz
Autograph picture
For multiple
Cincinnati Reds
World Series Championships.

**\*\*December 18, 2025\*\***
**\*\*41 years old\*\***

# Christmas Eve Ride Home

It's 11:15 P.M.
Have an hour-drive
On lonesome country roads
Still feeling jolly
After celebrating Christmas
With my in-laws
My wife is sound asleep
Our two-year-old son
Is locked on
A glowing light
Emerging from the stars

I keep my eyes
On the roads
As the glowing light
Descends
I
Notice something strange
There are no
Windows or wings
Only a steady red light
In front of a large sleigh
"It can't be," I exclaim

I slam on the brakes
I'm staring at
Santa and his reindeer
"Look, mommy,"
Our son says gleefully
She jolts awake
Rubs her eyes
Asks
"Am I seeing what
I think I'm seeing?"

Joe Tallarigo

I lock eyes with Santa
Knowing I must
Beat him to my house
To get my family into bed
To receive our presents
I put the pedal to the metal
Taking off down the road

It's a tie as
Santa and I arrive
In my neighborhood
Santa begins going down
Our neighbors chimneys

Giving
My wife and son
A few minutes
To set out
Cookies and milk
Get into bed

However our son
Is wide awake
Wants to meet Santa
Open his presents

It's Christmas Eve
Driving home
From my in-laws
My family getting
To see
Santa and his reindeer.

**December 8, 2019**
**34 years old**

# Merry Christmas, Little One

What a beautiful sight it is
Seeing the Christmas lights
Reflecting in your eyes
As snow falls gently outside
The embers in the fireplace
Are quickly dying out
Don't pout
Hot Chocolate
Will keep us warm
As we watch
Christmas specials on TV

I lean over and whisper
Merry Christmas, Little One

My little angel
In her favorite
Christmas sweater
Her golden hair
In a red bow
She can't wait
To play in the snow

All I can say is
Merry Christmas, Little One

She's now
at the tree
Spinning the ornaments
Looking at me
Laughing gleefully
Turning our house
Into
Christmas splendor

Joe Tallarigo

Grandfather clock
Chimes
Ten times
Her
Glowing Christmas light eyes
Are growing dim

Little One
It's
Time to get to bed
Let the
Sugar plum fairies
Dance in your head
Sleep tight
On this
Silent night

Santa
Will soon be here
I already have
The perfect gift

I whisper in your ear
Merry Christmas, Little One

Sleep tight
On this
Silent night
A Christmas
Now complete.

**December 1, 2009**
**24 years old**

(This is the 25th, poem in the book)

## Merry Christmas, Little One

Joe Tallarigo

# Donner Hill

Oh snow
Where are you
This young boy
Wants to take
His new sled
Race down Donner Hill
For a late December thrill

Santa
Finally came through
Bringing me the sled
The exact one
All my friends have

Now
I can join them
In fun sled racing
Seeing
Who's the fastest
To get to the bottom
of
Donners Hill

However
There's only
Brown grass, dead leaves
Leaving this young boy
With only
Winter day dreams
Racing down Donners Hill
Feeling the wind
Against my skin
In the
Bitter cold and snow

Oh snow
Where are you
There's only
A few days left
Of Christmas break
Would love to take
My new sled
Up to Donners Hill
Spending these days
Getting my thrill in
Before school starts again

With my luck
It'll finally snow
During a
January school day
Having to wait
'Til the school bell
Rings at three

Adding to my misery
As I'm about to leave
My teacher will stop us
Assign the class
Hours of homework

Leaving me
Just enough time
For
One or two rides
Down Donners Hill
For an
Early January thrill.

**November 26, 2025**
**40 years old**

Joe Tallarigo

# Santa's Here in Jamaica

Santa's here in Jamaica
Swapping cookies
For chicken wings
No more North Pole cold
He wants to enjoy
A warm tropical breeze

Spotlight hits his shiny coat
Red glow in the night
Crowds freeze, jaws drop low
Can't believe this sight

No more sleigh bells
Steel drums are in
Rudolph taps a beat
Santa spins Mrs. Claus
On the dance floor

Elves in flip-flops
Twist and shout
Amongst the palm trees
Draped in twinkling lights

Fireworks flare above the bay
Lanterns float in the wind
Santa roars in glee
The music soars
Shock spreads
Near and far

Coconut drinks in every hand
Volcano drinks ignite
Santa boogies, parrots cheer
Crowds frozen in sight

Sandcastles radiate
With candy lights
Elves toss presents wide
Santa's center stage all night
Shock and joy collide

Glitter flies from his coat
Spins and belly laughs
Never wants to stop
This
New Year's Eve party
Just might be better
Than
A Christmas party hop

Midnight strikes
The stars shining bright
Santa steals a kiss
From Mrs. Claus
The crowd applauds
At this loving sight

Sleigh parked
By a shimmering bay
Rudolph nods and bows
Santa tips his jolly hat
Leaving the crowd in shock

It's New Year's Eve
Santa trading in
Cookies for chicken wings
The cold and the snow
For
Tropical breezes and sand.

**December 10, 2019**
**34 years old**

# Chapter Three

# Nine O'clock Sunsets
# And
# Tropical Adventures

# Nine O'clock Sunsets

I'm not ready
To go inside
I can still feel
The warmth on my skin
I've been waiting
For this exact moment
Since last July

It's nine o'clock at night
The sun is still shining
High in the sky

Let's
Fire up the grill
I'll pour
Two shots of tequila
Toast to the fact
We're still outside
Having a good time
At
Nine o'clock at night

Let's transform
Our backyard
Into a tropical destination
Tiki torches all lit up
Stringed lights in the tree
Convert the shed into a bar
Serving the coldest drinks
While
Playing the hottest songs
From our new jukebox

What do you say

Joe Tallarigo

I'm not ready
To go inside
I can still feel
The warmth on my skin
I've been waiting
For this exact moment
Since last July

It's
Nine o'clock at night
The sun is still shining
High in the sky

There's
No snow or ice
The dogs
Can now enjoy
Their walks
My kids
Are still hyper
Chasing fireflies
The neighbors
Are also here
Eating all the food
Drinking all the beer

I tell you
It's paradise
With the sun
Now
Setting at
Nine o'clock.

**February 27, 2021**
**36 years old**

# A Little Bit Hotter

I don't mind
It's only
Seventy-five degrees
However
It's mid-July
My wife wants a tan
My kids need to
Play in the water
So, Mother Nature
Can you make it
a little bit hotter

Now Mother Nature
Don't roast or burn us
Keep the humidity low
There's no need
To go tropical
Though
I wouldn't mind
Cool ocean breezes
A bottle of tequila and rum
With
Endless clear blue skies

Kids pack up the car
Don't forget the
Sunscreen, picnic basket
Let's not waste time
Even though
We're
Going to stay out 'til nine
In this warm sunshine
Now that Mother Nature
Made it a little bit hotter

Joe Tallarigo

Now Mother Nature
Don't roast or burn us
Keep the humidity low
There's no need
To go tropical
Though
I wouldn't mind
Cool ocean breezes
A bottle of tequila and rum
With
Endless clear blue skies

Oh No
Mother Nature
Has betrayed us
Bringing relentless
Heat and humidity
For the next
Three weeks

Don't fret, family
I just saw on
The Weather Channel
It's snowing
In the Rocky Mountains
Let's pack our bags
Go celebrate
Christmas in July

Since
Mother Nature
Has made it
A whole lot hotter.

**April 19, 2019**
**34 years old**

# I'll See Your Sunrise

I see the dreams
You hold in your eyes
The ones you feel
Are impossible to chase
The ones you know
Don't happen overnight

Dreams that
A young woman like you
Says can only be found
In a fairytale paradise

I'll see your sunrise
Over island blue
First light
Falling through the room
Waking up every morning
To the sound of the waves
Your shadow dancing
On the wall like flames
We'll fall together
On the gritty sand
Declaring it our
Promise land

You've
Been running on
Calendars and dead ends
Time to call on a friend
Who knows you deep
Who can reach your soul
The one who can help you
Thake control
Of your dreams

Joe Tallarigo

I'll see your sunrise
Over island blue
First light
Falling through the room
Waking up every morning
To the sound of the waves
Your shadow dancing
On the wall like flames
We'll fall together
On the gritty sand
Declaring it our
Promise land

Our home
Will always
Have open windows
Let the night roll in slow
Hear guitars on the shoreline
Playing songs we almost know
I'll take you by the hand
Ask if I can have this dance
Our shadows swaying
On the wall like flames
My heart saying

If loving you
Means changing plans
I'll follow you
Wherever the ocean stands
Every dream
Starts where you are
I'll see your sunrise
No matter how far.

**December 26, 2025**
**41 years old**

# Days Don't Ask Your Name

I
Crave the freedom
Of feeling the
Warm winds in my sail
Pull up my rusty anchor
Hit the open road
Let my pirate soul
Lead me to a
Shanty beach town
Where they don't care
Where I come from

Out here
It's
Mango rum dinners
Key lime-pie breakfasts
Life feels lighter
When I feel it fade
Out here, the days
Don't ask your name
Turn the noise down
Let the ocean play
Let the tide
Decides what stays

I'm
fitting right in
Sailing in my boat
In the moonlight bay
Winking at all the girls
Phone turned off
Heart wide open
Every moment
Feels unbroken

Joe Tallarigo

Every mile back home
Is a thousand miles
Don't need any calendar
Hanging on my wall
I can be anyone
Out here, the days
Don't ask your name

Out here
It's
Mango rum dinners
Key lime-pie breakfasts
Life feels lighter
When I feel it fade
Out here, the days
Don't ask your name
Turn the noise down
Let the ocean play
Let the tide
Decides what stays

Seagulls in the air
Let freedom sway
If there's one thing
I came here to claim
Out here, the days
Don't ask your name
The sun goes down
The stars explain
Why I live life
Easier this way
I don't come here
To let freedom fade.

**December 26, 2025**
**41 years old**

# Red Sky Delight

Flip-flops in the sand
Sun slipping low
Let your worries go
Steel drums talking
To the ocean tide
Every color
Shows up for the ride

Palm trees lean in
Like they know a secret
Warm breeze humming
Like it's going to keep it

Red sky at night, delight
Bar tabs running high
DJ
Play me another song
Gonna dance
With every island girl
The mood is right
To see
Paradise in our eyes
Red sky at night, delight

There's
A bartender
Named Cosmo
Who knows my game
Pours a little heavy
I don't complain
The jukebox
Is firing up
Congo line forms
Keeping the party going

Joe Tallarigo

Lanterns glow
Laughter drifts out
Ukulele strums a sway so sweet
Moon rising to meet the beat

Red sky at night, delight
Bar tabs running high
DJ
Play me another song
Gonna dance
With every island girl
The mood is right
To see
Paradise in our eyes
Red sky at night, delight

Flip-flop philosophers
Gather around
Talking big dreams
'Til the ice melts down
Somebody's laughing
Somebody sings
Somebody swears
This place has wings

Barefoot dreams
Party soul
Seashell necklaces
Ocean humming
Boats sailing
Island girls swaying
It's going to be
A good time
Red sky at night, delight.

**December 28, 2025**
**41 years old**

# Anywhere With You

We have a road, no big hurry
Windows open, the day feels right
You're humming along to the radio
Laughing in the golden light
Boardwalk signs, postcard colors
We're going to have a blast
Every mile feels like magic
A day I want to last

No rush, no reason
Afternoon bliss
Every place is paradise
When
I'm riding with you

We'll go
Slow-mo, no plans, sunshine
Palm trees waving hello
Waves rolling in
Key Largo Heart, Montego dreams
A quiet pier at night
Winning boardwalk games
Just say the place
I'll go anywhere with you

Flip-flops tapping the sidewalk
Paper maps and silly turns
Small-town diners
Friendly faces
Every laugh
A memory earned
Every day is
Bright and simple
Every road is a wonderland

Joe Tallarigo

No clocks, no worries
Just a sky
So wide and blue
Grab my hand
Lead the way

We'll go
Slow-mo, no plans, sunshine
Palm trees waving hello
Waves rolling in
Key Largo Heart, Montego dreams
A quiet pier at night
Winning boardwalk games
Just say the place
I'll go anywhere with you

Maybe it's a
Beach town afternoon
Or a
Quiet street parade
Maybe it's a
Nowhere moment

As long as we're
Making these
Heartfelt moments
That's all I need
Every experience
Another page
To our love story.

**December 28, 2025**
**41 years old**

# Impulse

There's a boat
Named Impulse
Drifting by
White hull glowing
In the marina light
Owned by a guy
Who doesn't answer why
Just grins like he
Already won tonight

Everybody is
Rocking in the sand
Jukebox is
Playing everyone's
Favorite beach tunes
Some nights
You don't
overthink the truth
You just let it happen
On impulse

Impulse
It just feels right
One slow song
Turns into a long night
No planes, no ties, no excuses
Just a good mood breaking loose
Hold on tight
Let the moment hit us
Every good memory
Starts with
Impulse
Yes, it does
Impulse

Joe Tallarigo

Sun goes down
Drinks stay cold
Every laugh
Gets a little bolder
Strangers talk
Like they go way back

Dock lights hum
Water shines
We're right on time
Some things
You don't get to choose
They choose you
Like falling into
Impulse

Impulse
It just feels right
One slow song
Turns into a long night
No planes, no ties, no excuses
Just a good mood breaking loose
Hold on tight
Let the moment hit us
Every good memory
Starts with
Impulse
Yes, it does
Impulse

There's a boat
Named Impulse
Drifting by
Are you ready?

**December 28, 2025**
**41 years old**

# If You're Checking Your Watch

If you're
Checking your watch
You're
Doing this all wrong
If you're
Worrying about later
You
Won't stay too long

If your
Cold drink
Is getting warm
You're in your head
Your troubled thoughts
Will form into a
Tropical storm

If you don't have
Sand in your suit
Are you truly relaxing
Changing your mood

We're on Island time
After many boat drinks
You'll want to
Throw out all your troubles
To the morning tide
Then at midnight
Offer your
Calendar and watch
To the glowing moon
You'll come to the
Forgone conclusion
Life is an illusion

Joe Tallarigo

If you're complaining
It's raining too much
While sipping margaritas
Telling tall tales
Just remember
You could be in an office
Stuck in meetings all day

If your thoughts
Drift off to an ex-fiancée
Thinking about
How great it would be
To have her here
By your side
It might be time
To order a few rounds
Of tequila

There's no need to
Rush or worry
Or make plans

We're on Island time
After many boat drinks
You'll want to
Throw out all your troubles
To the morning tide
Then at midnight
Offer your
Calendar and watch
To the glowing moon
You'll come to the
Forgone conclusion
Life is an illusion.

**December 29, 2025**
**41 years old**

# Pink Flamingos

By the pool under the Summer sun
Pink flamingos glisten, having all the fun
Strutting slow, with a sway so sweet
Dancing on a lawn to a tropical beat

Sip a drink, kick back
Let your worries fade
We're living the good life
In the
Pink Flamingo parade

Pink Flamingo's
Sway with me
Barefoot on the
Snow-white sand
Feel the ocean breeze
Stand tall, stand proud
In a rosy glow
Life's a beach
Where the
Pink flamingos go

Tiptoe on one leg
Watch them sway
A splash of color
In the heat of the day
Twist your neck
Catch the rhythm slowly
Follow the flock
Where the trade winds blow

Sun on our face
We're enjoying life
In the Pink Flamingo space

Joe Tallarigo

Pink Flamingo's
Sway with me
Barefoot on the
Snow-white sand
Feel the ocean breeze
Stand tall, stand proud
In a rosy glow
Life's a beach
Where the
Pink flamingos go

When the sun dips low
We'll toast and cheer
Pink wings in moonlight
Paradise is here
Laughing loudly
As the tide rolls in slowly
Life is better with a
Pink flamingo show

Pink Flamingo's
Sway with me
Barefoot on the
Snow-white sand
Feel the ocean breeze
Stand tall, stand proud
In a rosy glow
Life's a beach
Where the
Pink flamingos go

Good vibes every day
Where the
Pink Flamingos go.

**December 29, 2025**
**41 years old**

# Pirate Hearts At Sea

Midnight sea waters call
Swords held up high
Stars playing in the sky
The moon, our flame
As we set sail

From
Tavern to tide
From
Port to shore
Every horizon
Is a new danger

Pirate hearts at sea
You and me
Staring down the enemy
No chains can bind
What the ocean stole
Two lovebirds
With pirate souls

We'll
Raid the docks
Claim
Treasures and doubloons
Chase
Shooting stars and silver moons
Dance
Through the storms

We'll never fall
Two lovebirds
Laughing at it all

Joe Tallarigo

Raise the Jolly Roger
Let the cannons roar
We'll steal the night
Leave the shores
With a wink and a laugh
We take the skies
Love is the treasure
In each other's eyes

Pirate hearts at sea
You and me
Staring down the enemy
No chains can bind
What the ocean stole
Two lovebirds
With pirate souls

Through cannon fire
Whispers of gold
It's your hand in mine
Let the wind chase us
Let the towns burn
Every port a story
Two love birds
Sparks flying
With every daring escape
We're meant to roam
Under endless Sky

Midnight sea waters call
Swords held up high
It's time to begin our night.

**December 29, 2025**
**41 years old**

# Dead Men Tell No Tales

The fog breathes thick
It crawls along the deck
Cold air
Encases the ship
Ghostly wisps
Swords in hands
Take shape
Demonic voices
Calling our names
Growling
Dead men tell no tales

Lightning parts the sky
Thunder roars like a cannon
A fierce wind blows
The ocean waves
Crash into the hull
A greenish portal swirls
Allowing the dead
To rise from the water
To take their revenge

The ghost crew
Raise their swords
Guttural AARS
Chill our bones
Stomping boots
Rush towards us
Sunken eyes
Out for blood
Metal against metal
Swords raging
In our fight
To staying alive

Joe Tallarigo

Lightning parts the sky
Thunder roars like a cannon
A fierce wind blows
The ocean waves
Crash into the hull
As we fight against
This ghostly crew
Who are out for revenge
It's a hellish sight

Our captain has lost control
We have no more fight
Our hands and feet are bound
The ghost captain
Grips the wheel
He wrenches it hard
Wood screams, iron moans
The sea comes alive
We're now spinning
Caught in a whirlpool
There's no hope
For survival tonight

The ghost captain
Cackles
"You're paying for your sins,"
As the ocean water
Gushes in
We're going
Down, down, down
Everything is growing
Darker.....

**December 29, 2025**
**41 years old**

# Squawk Back, Louie

Perched on the rail
With a feathered grin
Bright green wings
A laugh built in
Knows every secret
Hears every plan
Repeats them to every man
Captain says, "Steady"
Louie asks, "Why?"
Then laughs so hard
He almost falls from the sky

He doesn't swab decks
He doesn't stand watch
But he knows
Where the rum
Is stashed and stored
Steals the key
Sneaks out the rum
In a barrel drum

Squawk Back, Louie
Tell it again
Every word, but louder
My fine-feathered friend
Hears one thing once
Now
The whole ship knows
If there's trouble brewing
He's the instigator
Squawk Back, Louie
Night and day
Talk like a pirate
In a parrot way

Joe Tallarigo

Calls the cook "lazy."
Calls the mate "blind."
Calls the captain "Peter Pan."
To stir him up
Laughs at storms
Mocks the wind
Yells "abandon ship."
With a mischievous grin
Pours his bird feed
Into the stew
To improve the taste

He has no manners
He has no shame
Captain says
"He needs to walk the plank."
But Louie
Just flies away

Squawk Back, Louie
Tell it again
Every word, but louder
My fine-feathered friend
Hears one thing once
Now the whole ship knows
If there's trouble brewing
He's the instigator
Squawk Back, Louie
Night and day
Talk like a pirate
In a parrot way.

**December 30, 2025**
**41 years old**

# Turning Forty

Merle Haggard, Hank Jr
Jimmy Buffett
Each has songs
About turning forty
That I love listening to
Dreaming about
What it'll feel like
The day I turn forty
Now what's this

I'm surrounded by
Great friends and family
Singing
Happy birthday to me
I count forty candles
On my chocolate cake
Surely
This is a big mistake

I still feel twenty-five
Lightning in my veins
Warm winds
Still catch my sail
I'm not even close
To throw in the flag
I'd rather raise it
I'm only getting started

Tropical paradises await me
Moonlight kisses, warm embraces
Boat drinks, gumbo
Watching a firework show
In Montego Bay
With the
Girl of my dreams

Joe Tallarigo

You know
I've had many
Trips around the sun
Always on the run
Still enjoy
Writing my songs
Midnight comes
I'm still on fire

I still feel twenty-five
Lightning in my veins
Warm winds
Still catch my sail
I'm not even close
To throw in the flag
I'd rather raise it
I'm only getting started

Though lately
I've been noticing
Time is moving fast
More important now
To make
Every moment last
You can't make
New memories
With the past

You can't
Make new memories
With the past.

**December 30, 2025**
**41 years old**

(This is the 40<sup>th</sup> poem in the book)

# I'm A Lighthouse

I'm a lighthouse
I was poured in stone
On this restless shore
Back when names
Still mattered more
They built me tall
So the lost and fearful
Can see me
In a turbulent sea

I've seen the sons
Take their father's place
Same brave eyes
Same stubborn face
Hearts set out
With a
Prayer and grin
Some make it back
Some give in

Ever alone
I do my part
With
A loving heart
I stay lit
When the
Moon and stars
Give up
When the
Waves throw a fit
Hope seems lost
I don't move, I don't run
I shine
'Til my work is done

Joe Tallarigo

I've heard
Confessions in the fog
Promises whispered to God
The weeping, the cursing
The cheers, the celebrations
The goodbyes, the hellos

I stay lit
for the
lost and scared
for the ones
who thought nobody cared
I don't speak, I don't fight
I bravely hold the line
With a faithful shine

I don't choose
Who makes it home
I don't choose
Who dies alone
My job is to turn
Slow and true
Hoping my light
Reaches you

I stay lit
Even when
The world moves on
When
I'm called outdated
I don't need thanks
I don't need praise
I faithfully burn through
The endless haze.

**December 30, 2025**
**41 years old**

# Good Time Fund

Orange spills on the bay
Is it morning, is it night
Is it Monday or Friday
I really can't say
I've been partying
What seems like weeks
On this
No name beach

Cozying up to the locals
Burning holes in my wallet
Saying
"Bartender, another round
For my new friends
It's Five O'clock somewhere."

I'm blowing through
My good-time fund
I started
When I was twenty-one
Time to live it up
Time for endless fun
With
Sunset kisses, sand, and rum

Barbecue eats
Steel drum beats
Locals dancing down
These sandy streets
Having so much fun
We don't know
If we're
Coming or going
In the hot tropical sun

Joe Tallarigo

There's a
Barefoot singer
With a
Beat-up guitar
Playing songs
About chasing dreams
I give him a twenty

He says
"Brother wears your map
Where are you bound?"
I grin
"Right here, where
Good times are found."

I'm blowing through
My good-time fund
I started
When I was twenty-one
Time to live it up
Time for endless fun
With
Sunset kisses, sand, and rum

Some choose fame
Some chase money
I chase good times
On beaches
With no names
With
Good people, good music
Where the days run together
The Summer lasts forever.

**May 23, 2019**
**34 years old**

# It's Raining, Must Be Thursday

It's raining, must be Thursday
Neon buzzing by the door
Puddles in the parking lot
Bartender pouring drinks
Friends enter smiling
Sharing new life updates
Old guitars still strumming
Loud minute-long applause
Even the thunder roars
One more Hank song

Wind Howling down
West Eighth Street
Shaking signs
In here
We're dry and performing
Let the weather
Do its worst again

It's raining, must be Thursday
Open mic and six strings
Our Nashville dreams
Won't be deterred
By this shouting storm
Trying to cross a line
We'll play on
'Til our voices are gone
Or
The power goes out

Tonight
In this little bar
It's nothing
But good times

Joe Tallarigo

There's a girl
With a notebook
Full of lines about
Finding her place in this world

There's a boy
With his usual hooks
Full of lines about
Drinking and fishing

There's
A Man and a  woman
Full of joy
Singing duets
To get the crowd's mind
Off the raging storm

It's raining, must be Thursday
Open mic and six strings
Our Nashville dreams
Won't be deterred
By this shouting storm
Trying to cross a line
We'll play on
'Til our voices are gone
Or
The power goes out

Tonight
In this little bar
It's nothing
But good times.

**\*\*April 20, 2019\*\***
**\*\*34 years old\*\***

# More Trips Around The Sun

Sun's glow is getting dimmer
The nightlife is getting shorter
Flip-flops, sunscreen, sunglasses
Are being stored away
The seashells we collected
Hang in your living room

The
Fourth of July celebration
On our tropical vacation
Where we saw fireworks
In each other's eyes
Is now a distant memory

Oh girl
What a Summer it's been
Our love growing
Brighter, stronger
Maybe it's these
Changes in latitudes
Changing my attitude
I'm thinking
Our short Summer together
Isn't enough
If you catch my drift

I want more
Trips around the sun
With you by my side
Chasing boardwalk dreams
Watching sunrises on the pier
Building our castle in the sand
Cold drinks in our hands
Sailing off to a distant shore

Joe Tallarigo

Cold Canadian winds
Are replacing these
Warm tropical breezes
I already miss
Hearing your laughter
Running barefoot
On white sandy beaches
Seeing your eyes glow
As I tried the local cuisine
Knowing what it meant to you

Oh girl
What a Summer it's been
Our love growing
Brighter, stronger
Maybe it's these
Changes in latitudes
Changing my attitude
I'm thinking
Our short Summer together
Isn't enough
If you catch my drift

I want more
Trips around the sun
With you by my side
Chasing boardwalk dreams
Watching sunrises on the pier
Building our castle in the sand
Cold drinks in our hands
Sailing off to a distant shore.

**December 31, 2025**
**41 years old**

# My Margaritaville

The sky above
Has its own
Shade of blue
The waters calm
As I daydream
'Neath that
Sky of blue

The kids splashing
Diving for the ball
Don't bother me at all
They're
Just having fun
The same fun
My brother and I
Had here
When we were kids

In the corner
Hangs a clock
I pay it
No attention
Time drifts slowly
When

Talking to good friends
Eating pizza and snacks
Drinking pop and beer
Laughing loudly
Saying hello
To everyone walking by
Drifting aimlessly
On these
Clear-blue waters

Joe Tallarigo

The midnight swim
Soothes my restless soul
Watching the lights
Dance on the water
Swimming 'neath
An endless dark sky
Full of shining stars
Almost surreal
How calm and relaxing
It can be
Drifting in this pool
As others are asleep

It's
A time capsule
Hearing the same songs
Playing over the speakers
I heard playing as a kid
Walking on the
same rugged blue carpet
in the stairways

Philipps Swim Club
Is my Margaritaville
Here in Price Hill
A five-minute drive
From my house
I could
Spend all day
Up there
Never getting bored
Or
Growing old.

**\*\*December 31, 2025\*\***
**\*\*41 years old\*\***

# My Margaritaville

**(The Pool)**

**(My Brother and Me)**
**(1990s)**

Joe Tallarigo

# Jimmy Buffett Tribute

There's
A new kind of emptiness
Blowing in off the Gulf
Legendary
Singer and performer
Jimmy Buffett
Has passed away
Just before
The Big Labor Day Show
Come Monday
We'll still be grieving

What will we do
when Summer comes
With no new Buffett song
No new soundtrack for Summer
To sing and drink along to
It's depressing to think
There are no more
All day tailgating parties
No more legendary shows

This
Doesn't seem real
Seems like
It's a bad dream
Wanting to wake up
To find
Jimmy Buffett
Is still with us
Sailing in the Tropics
Working on new songs
Announcing His
Legendary Summer tours

What will we do
when Summer comes
With no new Buffett song
No new soundtrack for Summer
To sing and drink along to
It's depressing to think
There are no more
All day tailgating parties
No more legendary shows

Thank you for sharing
Your poetic soul
Bringing the
Laid-back tropical lifestyle
To every
Song and concert
Your
Summer never ends
Positive attitude
Allowing everyone
To be part of
Margaritaville

Now
When it's
Five o'clock
We'll
Raise a cold one
Sing along
To all your songs
We'll sing along.

**\*\*June 22, 2024\*\***
**\*\*39 years old\*\***

# Chapter 4

# Laissez les bons temps rouler
# With
# Mardi Gras and Bayou Magic

# Cajun Crocodile Stomp

There's a hot new act
Taking over
The Louisiana Swamps
A crocodile wearing
A purple cowboy hat
Who plays the accordion

Can you believe that
A crocodile wearing
A purple cowboy hat
Leading
The Cajun Crocodile Stomp

"Are you feeling alright?"
He asks the crowd
I see you're in disbelief
Watching

A crocodile wearing
A purple cowboy hat
Who plays the accordion
Teaching you the steps to
The Cajun Crocodile Stomp

Dr. John
May he rest in peace
Taught me the secrets
To the Zydeco beats
Must feel
The music in your soul
The rhythm will grab you
'Neath a Cajun Moon
Clap your hands, stomp your feet
Spin around, do it again

Joe Tallarigo

Come on
Boys and girls
Get your groove on
Don't fret

That I'm a crocodile
Wearing
A purple cowboy hat
Leading
The Cajun Crocodile Stomp

If it
Begins to rain
The wind howls
Keep on swaying
I'm
Going to keep on playing
So you can dance to

The hottest music craze
Taking over
The Louisiana Swamps
Called
The Cajun Crocodile Stomp

There's a hot new act
Taking over
The Louisiana Swamps
A crocodile wearing
A purple cowboy hat
Who plays the accordion
Leading
The Cajun Crocodile Stomp.

**\*\*June 10, 2019\*\***
**\*\*34 years old\*\***

# Daughter Of The Cajun Land

She proclaims
I have Mississippi water
Flowing through my veins
I grew up playing
In the Delta mud
I'm finally twenty-one
Attending my
First Mardi Gras
Honoring my heritage
Carrying on my family's
New Orleans traditions
Celebrating our culture

My Grandma
Is a voodoo queen
Can heal or curse you
Mama is a homemaker
Makes the spiciest gumbo
Papa plays the piano
In a Zydeco band
My name is Jessi
A proud daughter
Of the Cajun Land

Look at all these
Cajun Kings lining up
Using their
Southern charm
Trying to make me
Their Cajun Queen
But
They're out of luck
This Cajun Queen
Flies solo

Joe Tallarigo

My Grandma
Is a voodoo queen
Can heal or curse you
Mama is a homemaker
Makes the spiciest gumbo
Papa plays the piano
In a Zydeco band
My name is Jessi
A proud daughter
Of the Cajun Land

Now
Under the Creole Moon
She makes her move
Putting the Cajun King
She's been eyeing
Under a love spell
Leads him down
Decatur Street
Say's
"I've got big plans
For you and me
Come meet my family."

My Grandma
Is a voodoo queen
Can heal or curse you
Mama is a homemaker
Makes the spiciest gumbo
Papa plays the piano
In a Zydeco band
My name is Jessi
A proud daughter
Of the Cajun Land.

**August 8, 2018**
**33 years old**

# Secrets Of New Orleans
## (Part One)

Moonlight bends
Where shadows gather
Iron lace breathing
Ancient sins
Boot heels echo
Where pirates bargained
Rum, blood oaths, safety
Mississippi River hums
Like a warning drum

Low and slow
Beneath the street
Every cobblestone remembers
All who vanished
In the dead of night

Throw the beads
Hide your fears tonight
Painted smiles
Cursed forever
Under candlelight
Every mask
Tells a different lie
Where the spirits
Walk in borrowed time
Witches conjure
Pirates still plunder

If you want to know
What darkness still survives
Follow the Secrets
Of New Orleans
In the night

Joe Tallarigo

Voodoo Queens
In shadowed doorways
Salt and bones
In silver bowls
There's a shipwreck
Buried in the Delta mud
Still ringing with
The crew's moan

Ghosts still dance
To the Zydeco beat
Hexes are tied
With carnival string
The river bends
But never forgets
Who loved, who died

Throw the beads
Hide your face tonight
Truth gets drunk
On wine and candlelight
Every painted mask
Slips before sunrise
The saints
Start naming names
Witches screech
Pirates sing shanties

You don't find
This city's heart
It finds you
And never parts.

**January 4, 2026**
**41 years old**

# Come Dance With The Ghosts

Lucky gris-gris bags
Jingling in time
With the Zydeco Beat
French Quarter Moon
Has the night on its feet
Neon signs say
"Come play."
Hot brass blowing
Through old blue flames

Beads flying everywhere
Shadows laughing low
Every crooked alley
Has a story to show
Gas lights flicker
Footsteps start following
A cold wind blows
The Cajun Beat grows louder
A whispering voice
says

Come dance with the ghosts
'Til the sun comes up
In the historic streets
Where the Zydeco rolls
The blues run free
The living and the dead
Move so easily
The night never rests
Neither do we
When New Orleans
Sings in the key
Of
"Haunt me"

Joe Tallarigo

Accordion crying
Like it's seen it all
Washboard rattling down
An old brick wall
A lady in white
Steps onto the stage
Hums a haunted tune

The spotlight glitches
She's gone in a mist
River fog claps to a
Four-four time
Mississippi grinning
Like it knows the rhyme

A spirit tips his hat
Says "Mind the groove."
Don't break the spell
Just let it move

Come dance with the ghosts
'Til the sun comes up
In the historic streets
Where the Zydeco rolls
The blues run free
The living and the dead
Move so easily
The night never rests
Neither do we
When New Orleans
Sings in the key
Of
"Haunt me"

**\*\*January 1, 2026\*\***
**\*\*41 years old\*\***

# It's Mardi Gras Time Again

Beads in the air
Falling heavily as a
Purple-green rain
King cake crumbs
On my shirt again

Streetcar riders humming
Drums shake the streets
Second line finds me
Women sure are frisky
Everyone
Pushing their way
To the front
To get the best seat

Balconies rocking
Music all around
Somebody yells "cher."
Plastic cups raised
No one knows the time
If you lost your voice
You're doing just fine

It's
Mardi Gras time again
Put on my mask
Blend in with
this party crowd
Let the good times roll
From sunrise beads
To moonlight soul
We'll be celebrating
The only way
New Orleans knows how

Joe Tallarigo

Brass bands spin
Block to block
Don't ever stop
Kids on ladders
Kings and Queens
Masks make heroes
Out of carnival dreams

Good times stronger
Than we planned
Found new friends
Holding both my hands

It's
Mardi Gras time again
Put on my mask
Blend in with
this party crowd
Let the good times roll
From sunrise beads
To moonlight soul
We'll be celebrating
The only way
New Orleans knows how

Purple, green, gold
In the streetlight glow
Even the sidewalks
Know where to go
Everybody singing
The wrong words loudly
Saints and sinners
In the same
Dang crowd.

**January 1, 2026**
**41 years old**

116

# The Bar Is Rocking

I'm
Counting my nickels
I'm
Counting my dimes
Gonna go down
To the corner bar
Feed the jukebox
'Til closing time

The bar will be
Rocking all night
Drinks
will be flowing
The neon
will be glowing
It's going to be
One hell of a show
I'm throwing a party
That spans
A country mile wide

Here comes
Zydeco Jolie
Gonna
Show the crowds
How to dance
To the
Rocking Zydeco Beat
Go Jolie Go
You're doing just fine
The spotlight
Is all yours
Get these crawdads
Onto the dance floor

Joe Tallarigo

The bar is rocking
Drinks are flowing
The neon is glowing
The dance floor is full
Cars are still pulling in
Someone proclaims
"They're coming from
Two counties over"

Bartender yells
"Last Call."
As Dr. John plays

I say
"I still have
Four more bags
Full of change
What do you say
We come back
Tomorrow night
Do it all again

The bar will be
Rocking all night
Drinks will be flowing
Neon will be glowing
It's going to be
One hell of a show
I'm throwing a party
That spans
A country mile wide.

**January 3, 2026**
**41 years old**

# You Don't Need Any Spells

You don't need any charms
You don't need any spells
You don't need any chants
You definitely
Don't need any rituals
To get to my heart

All you need is
Your sweet composure
Your good time spirit
Your loving smile
To get to my heart

You've got me
Soaring high
People can see it
In my eyes
I'm a lucky guy
As we hold hands
Walking down
The street
To the plans
That we made

You're dancing
To the music
Browsing through the
Trinkets, stones, beads
You think you need
To get to my heart

You move on
To each booth
Wondering what to buy

Joe Tallarigo

I say
"Take your time
There's no place
I'd rather be."

But honey
Don't spend your money
On these things
Buy yourself
A necklace, dog, or cat

You don't need any charms
You don't need any spells
You don't need any chants
You definitely
Don't need any rituals
To get to my heart

All you need is
Your sweet composure
Your good time spirit
Your loving smile
To get to my heart

You've got me
Soaring high
People can see it
In my eyes
I'm a lucky guy
As we hold hands
Walking down
The street
To the plans
That we made.

**January 3, 2026**
**41 years old**

# Haunted Lands

Thick fog
Encases
Every grave
Hiding the names
Of those spirits
Moaning and wailing

High above
Dozens of crows
Cawing and circling
They're on night duty
Keeping an eye out
For the living

Church bells toll
A haunting
Midnight tune
Alerting the dead
It's time to rise
To haunt these lands

In muddy waters
Moss-draped crocodiles
Line the shores
Teeth ready to bite
Protecting their homes
From the living

Dark shadows
Dart from tree to tree
Looking to possess
Anyone who dares
Enter these
Haunted Lands

Joe Tallarigo

On dead branches
Hollow-eyed owls
Make their plans
For swooping down
On the living

Strange lights
Hover in the bayou
Guiding lost souls
To the witch
Who dwells there

In the tree lines
Smoke-black bats
Swarm like storm clouds
Spill down attacking
On the living

Blood-red moon
Hangs silently above
The guiding light
Beating soul
Of the underworld

In the brush
Red-eyed hell hounds
Gnash and growl
Attacking and snacking
On the living.

**January 3, 2026**
**41 years old**

# One Neon Night

One neon night
All the words
All the strumming
Will come together
The crowd will recognize
Something special
Is happening here

They'll stand up
Put their beers down
Draw closer to the stage
To see the face
Who's been singing
Their songs regularly
For the past year

One neon night
The crowds gather
Near the exit
Pens and paper waving
Everyone wanting
The singer's autograph
It's becoming clear

After each set
The singer
No longer
Has to pay
For their own beer
The fans ship in
Just keep playing
You're our hero

Joe Tallarigo

One neon night
The bar is full
Standing room only
The spotlight
Feels hotter
It's almost showtime
The crowd cheering

The singer
Starts to strum
The crowd erupts
Flashes of light
Light up the dim bar
The singer goes all in
It feels surreal

They get
Lost in the songs
They get
Lost in the crowd
The words
Rolling off their tongue
Can anyone hear

One neon night
All the words
All the strumming
Will come together
The crowds will
Cheer you on
All your dreams
Coming true
It's your year.

**January 3, 2026**
**41 years old**

# Zydeco Simon

Zydeco Simon
Wore his Sunday best
On a Tuesday night
Pocket full of beads
A bottle of good times
They say he danced
Past the break of dawn
When the band packed up
Simon kept on

Mississippi mist
In his hair so fine
Laughs like thunder
He wants to
Keep dancing
Be it a
Sad Waltz or Rocking Zydeco
He doesn't care

Zydeco Simon
Shake the floor
Even the dead
Want one more dance
Ghosts in the corner
With Mardi Gras grins
Rattle those bones
Let the night cave in
If the band stops playing
He doesn't mind
He'll stomp
In afterlife time
Zydeco Simon
Still wants to
Party tonight

Joe Tallarigo

Hear the accordion
Cry low and moan
Telling tales
You haven't seen
Tambourine pulsates
As a fast heartbeat
Brass horns blowing
The Devil's heat

Zydeco Simon
On the dance floor
Spinning a girl
Who also likes
To dance all night
The perfect couple
Whose laughter
Fills the halls
Long after it closes

Zydeco Simon
Shake the floor
Even the dead
Want one more dance
Ghosts in the corner
With Mardi Gras grins
Rattle those bones
Let the night cave in
If the band stops playing
He doesn't mind
He'll stomp
In afterlife time
Zydeco Simon
Still wants to
Party tonight.

**January 5, 2026**
**41 years old**

# You're My Sun On Rainy Days

You're my sun on rainy days
Burning through the cold and gray
Rays beam from your heart
Lighting up the world
That has drifted away
So long ago

The smile on your face
Says, "I'm safe here"
I can proudly proclaim
I've seen rain falling
On sunny days

Wet streets hum
Like an old love song
We sing along
Making up our own words
A perfect duet
Two hearts in sync
On such a dreary day

You're the only girl
Who I'd love to twirl
In the pouring rain
As thunder rolls
The wind
Striking up leaves
Blowing them
Straight at us
As
Lightning strikes
The fields of gold
Setting them
Aflame

Joe Tallarigo

You're my sun on rainy days
Burning through the cold and gray
Rays beam from your heart
Lighting up the world
That has drifted away
So long ago

The smile on your face
Says, "I'm safe here"
I can proudly proclaim
I've seen rain falling
On sunny days

Rain
Keep on falling
You're only
Charging her up
Setting her heart aglow
Her smile starts to grow
A loving feeling
Stirs in my soul

I take you in my arms
Keep on twirling you
Showing the world
That has drifted away
So long ago
I'm carrying on
With the girl
Who's my sun
On these
Rainy days.

**January 6, 2026**
**41 years old**

# Séance On The Bayou

They weren't brave
They were bored

That's how it begins
In places like this
Where the road ends
The mossy bayou
Finishes the journey

Six teens
Form a circle
Join hands
Start chanting
In a haunted tone
Calling out
Spirits names

Casey says
"We know
You're here."
Stacey Demands
"Come on, spirits
Just appear
We're not scared."

A hexed moon
Begins rising
Above
The Cyprus Trees
Stopping dead
Right above them
Hanging there
Like a
Bad omen

Joe Tallarigo

Branches begin
To snap all around
Ghostly wails
Carry in the wind
Owls begin to screech
Bat wings flutter
This mossy bayou
Has come alive
As
Red-eyed shadows
Rise above
The muddy waters

The teens tremble
At this haunted scene
The red-eyed shadows
Hums a gothic lament
As they give chase

The bayou
Twists and turns
As the teens run
Ending up
Where they began
Staring straight
Into the red eyes

Hexed moon
Shines bright
On the teens
Can you hear
Their screams?

**January 6, 2026**
**41 years old**

130

# For My Aunt Sue
## (Part One)

The morning welcomes me with
Misty rain and thick fog
Bourbon is still asleep
Neon signs don't glow
I'm lost in my thoughts
A strong scent of
Cigarette smoke
Makes me turn my head
A ghostly hand takes mine
Hear you say
"Let's walk, my friend"

You always loved this town
Always wanted to see
New Orleans
Through your eyes
A personal tour
That only you would know
To make any stranger
Feel like they belong
Here in this city
Of good times and magic

Take me to the bars
Where
Jazz and the blues
Still reign king
Let the music remind us
How it used to be
Every Summer and Spring
You know
I loved attending
Those shows with you

131

Joe Tallarigo

If the music gets too loud
We can move to a small café
There's so much
I want to tell you
There's so much
I need to say

You know I was
Mad and blue
When you
Received your wings
Didn't know
What I was going to do
How was I going to go on
Without you by my side
Who was I going to call
When life got me down
You always gave me good advice
I always enjoyed calling you
With the exciting news
Of every singer
Coming to town

Somehow
I pulled through
Putting pen to paper
Writing songs
About your passing
Using allusions
Of New Orleans
To help me deal
To feel what you felt
From your stories here
With Uncle Dave.

**January 5, 2026**
**41 years old**

# For My Aunt Sue
## (Part One)

**(My Uncle Dave and Aunt Sue)**

Hi Joe,
Having a great time.
the weather is beautiful.
We are so relaxed.
Talk to you on
Tuesday.
Love,
Sue + Dave

**(Postcard from my Aunt Sue and Uncle Dave
From New Orleans)**

Joe Tallarigo

# For My Aunt Sue
## (Part Two)

You always loved this town
Always wanted to see
New Orleans
Through your eyes
A personal tour
That only you would know
To make any stranger
Feel like they belong
Here in this city
Of good times and magic

We drift down
Street to street
Letting you do
All the talking
About all your good times
Pointing out all the venues
You frequented

You and Uncle Dave
Were always
Personally proud
Having your names
Etched on
Personal barstools
In Margaritaville

I can only imagine
All the fun
You two had
Throwing back cold ones
Swapping stories
With your friends
In the glow of neon

Isn't it weird
We lived in Cincinnati
Yet
New Orleans
The city of
Jazz, spells, magic
Is where we chose
To reunite
You, a ghost
I'm still living

Even now
At the age
Of forty-one
I still want to
Experience all that
New Orleans
Has to offer
To walk the streets
With you
Like we planned to

You always loved this town
Always wanted to see
New Orleans
Through your eyes
A personal tour
That only you would know
To make any stranger
Feel like they belong
Here in this city
Of good times and magic.

**January 5, 2026**
**41 years old**

# For My Aunt Sue
## (Part Two)

**(My Aunt Sue and Me)**

**(My Uncle Dave, Me, and Aunt Sue)**

# Secrets Of New Orleans
## (Part Two)

Who's roaming
The cobblestone streets
At three A.M.
Is it
A curious tourist
With adventurous eyes
Or is it
A restless spirit
Looking for a good time

Do the church bells ring
For the living or the dead
Are those prayers
Or words unsaid

Is
Jean Lefitte's treasure
Real or just a legend
A pirate story
To pass the time
On moonless nights
Do the vampires sleep
When the daylight breaks
Or
Just close their eyes
For the city's sake

Is every
New Orleans
Dark and old secrets
Being holed up
Or are
they being told

Joe Tallarigo

What's that whisper
Coming off the cards
Is it the truth
Or something pulled
From the dark
Why do fortune tellers
Smile the way they do
Like they already saw
Tomorrow's fate

If New Orleans
Calls your name
Is it luck, is it fame
Or is it fate
Leading you to
A dark truth

If we ever discover
The Secrets of New Orleans
They won't come clean
They won't come easily
They're rooted in voodoo
Cemetery dreams
In red-blood moons
And accordions

I'll bet my soul
For what I believe
The dark still convenes
On every back street
Here in
New Orleans.

**January 4, 2026**
**41 years old**

# Chapter Five

# I Want To Write You
# A
# Country Music Love Song

Joe Tallarigo

# Country Music Love Song

I want to write you
A Country Music love song
But
Everything about love
Has been written
Under the sun

From
"Good Morning Beautiful"
"Tonight, I Want To Be Your Man"
I guess I'll have to
Come up with a new plan

The words I want to say
Lonestar sang in "Amazed"
"I'm Wrapped Around"
"Wrapped Up In You"
Have been sung by
Brad Paisley and Garth Brooks
Guess it's back to the books
For a new hook

"I Cross My Heart"
Is sung by George Strait
"How Forever Feels"
is a Kenny Chesney song

I wish
Someone would leave me
An idea and a hook
So I can tell you
How I feel about
You
In my own special way

 I made up a tune
Soon discovered
It sounded like
Clint Black's
"When I Said I Do"

"I'll Go On Loving You"
Alan Jackson Declares
"It's Your Love"
Is a beautiful duet
By
Faith Hill and Tim McGraw

What about the line
When You Say Nothing At All
Now, that's a beautiful song
By the great Keith Whitley
Guess it's going to take me
All Summer and Fall
To write you a love song

Maybe
I'll make you
A playlist
With all the songs
I've mentioned
Then
Relax in my favorite chair
Turn down the lights
Pour some wine
Hey those sound
Like great lines
Just kidding….

**March 23, 2014**
**29 years old**

Joe Tallarigo

# Say Hello

So far away
So I say a prayer
That one day
Our
Path will cross

You're
A stranger
Across the street
An alluring girl
With no name
How can I
Get us to meet
So I can say
Hello

How fun it would be
Walking in the parks
Taking in the arts
Cheering on our
Favorite sports teams
Having candlelight dinners
On midnight cruises

There's
So much
We can do
Life and love
Wouldn't be
So boring
If only
I could say
Hello

Should I
Leave it up to fate
Or
Take the first chance
I get
To cross the street
Introduce myself
And say
Hello

How fun it would be
Walking in the parks
Taking in the arts
Cheering on our
Favorite sports teams
Having candlelight dinners
On midnight cruises

There's
So much
We can do
Life and love
Wouldn't be
So boring
If only
I could say
Hello

Hello
One little word
Yet
So hard to say
To a girl like you.

**October 10, 2013**
**28 years old**

Joe Tallarigo

# Sing Me A Song

Down by the river
On a moon-filled night
Just you and me
A gentle breeze blows
Fireflies dance in a line
A sparkle in your eyes
That's speaking to me

Saying
Sing me a song
Sing about
Love and magic
Sing about
Summer nights
Riverside vows
How this girl
Should be loved
Sing me a song
A song about
You and me

Feel the rhythm
Of the water
As it flows by
Watch the stars
As they
Twinkle in formation
Listen to the
Hooting owls
In the trees
One by one
They're
Speaking to me

Saying
Sing a song
Sing about
Love and magic
Sing about
Summer nights
Riverside vows
How that girl
Should be loved
Sing a song
Sing about
You and her

We're
Two young hearts
Falling in love
Here in the dark
Here in the country
Your eyes shining

Saying
Sing me a song
Sing about
Love and magic
Sing about
Summer nights
Riverside vows
How this girl
Should be loved
Sing me a song
A song about
You and me.

**May 5, 2009**
**24 years old**

Joe Tallarigo

# Love Thang

We're hopeless romantics
With wild-scheme dreams
Trying to win the hearts of
The women we believe
Who will be our queens
Having a few kids
To add to our family tree

We believe in
Love at first sight
Having dinner by candlelight
We enjoy slow dancing
Making midnight magic
Going on romantic getaways
Having your mother stay with us

It's
A love thang
A code we live by
Us guys
Must take a stand
Prove
That we're in it
Until the end
Having good times
With our wives
We enjoy
Hugging and kissing
As much
As we like
Hunting and fishing
It's
A love thang

We like
Wishing upon stars
Driving fast cars
Writing songs on guitars
Walking our dogs
In the park

We enjoy
Sipping
Homemade sweet tea
On front porch swings
Working hard, taking overtime
To buy our girl
The perfect engagement ring

It's
A love thang
A code we live by
Us guys
Must take a stand
Prove
That we're in it
Until the end
Having good times
With our wives
We enjoy
Hugging and kissing
As much
As we like
Hunting and fishing
It's
A love thang.

**\*\*February 22, 2003\*\***
**\*\*18 years old\*\***

Joe Tallarigo

# Wild Wild Dreams

I
Have a showdown
At sundown
With an old memory
A few rounds of whiskey
And I'm sound asleep

Having
Wild wild dreams
Of the
Wild Wild West
Searching
For a girl
Who left me
Many moons ago
For an outlaw
Who stole her away
In a Texas tornado
Leaving me
Broken hearted

Her wanted poster
Hangs on my heart
Her blue eyes
Pierce the night
Her soft voice
Carries in the wind
Her words faint
Not knowing
What she's saying
All I know is
When
I fall asleep

I'm
Having
Wild wild dreams
Of the Wild Wild West
Searching
For a girl
Who left me
Many moons ago
For an outlaw
Who stole her away
In a Texas tornado
Leaving me
Broken hearted

In my
Wild wild Dreams
Of the
Wild Wild West

I
Don't care
How long
It will take
Don't care
How long
I ride
Once we reunite
Win back her heart
We'll
Ride off into the sunset
Of the
Wild Wild West
In my
Wild wild dreams.

**February 3, 2005**
**20 years old**

149

Joe Tallarigo

# If Love Were Like A Movie

If love
Were like a movie
We'd
Fall in love at first sight
Stumble over our words
Getting to the first hello
Trying to keep our composure
Exchanging our phone numbers

As we walk away
We'll secretly
Look back at each other
Knowing
We're meant to be

If love
Were like a movie
We'd go on a few dates
Talking all night
Making plans
For a weekend getaway
Getting to know
Each other's
Quirky little habits

If love
Were like a movie
We'd end up
In a big fight
Yelling
Hateful things
We don't mean
Walking out the door
With no end in sight

Both ending up
Crying and moping
Waiting for one of us
To swallow
Our foolish pride

But
Weeks later
We'll meet by chance
Reconciling our love
As if nothing
Bad happened
Between us

If love
Were like a movie
I know
How it would end

We'd
Live happily ever after
Having
What we always wanted
When we first met
Having to wait
Until the
Final scene
For us to be
Together forever.

**\*\*August 20, 2009\*\***
**\*\*24 years old\*\***

Joe Tallarigo

# She Makes My World Go Round

My world can be
Troubled and deep
When
I
Don't see her
In days

I
Can't sleep
I'm
Jittery and weak
Can't eat
Makes for a bad day
Until I see
Her loving smile
On her face
Then
I'm back
In my happy place

She makes
My world go round
She doesn't
Have to do much
To get
My heart racing
When we sit
By each other
Nothing else matters
She can stay still
Not make any  sound
To make
My world go round

She's
Got something special
It all seems magical
The way we connect
Not as lovers
More like soul mates
Until
The end of time
She's my best friend
Who keeps me in line

She makes
My world go round
She doesn't
Have to do much
To get
My heart racing
When we sit
By each other
Nothing else matters
She can stay still
Not make any  sound
To make
My world go round.

**\*\*April 26, 2010\***
**\*\*25 years old\*\***

Joe Tallarigo

# Long Way To Houston
## (Duet)

You hold the key
To my young heart
Which holds all my
Secrets and fears

To tell you the truth
Love hasn't been
On my mind for years

Now
all my dreams
One-way streets
Are leading me
To the start
Of something new
And it's all
Thanks to you

It's
A long way
To Houston
Where we always said
We would meet
In the middle
To start life anew
I still have
Hours to go
Until
I see
The Houston skyline
Until
I hold you in my arms
Once again

Love is a funny thing
When you fall in deep
I never knew
What a man could do
To this
Young woman's heart

These California boys
Have nothing on you
Chasing waves
Chasing Hollywood Dreams
Is not for me

Now
I'm on the road
To something new
It's leading me
Straight to you

 It's
A long way
To Houston
Where we always said
We would meet
In the middle
To start life anew
I still have
Hours to go
Until
I see
The Houston skyline
Until
I hold you in my arms
Once again.

**\*\*June 1, 2006\*\***
**\*\*21 years old\*\***

Joe Tallarigo

# Stars On My Walls

There are stars
On my walls
Heaven above
In the velvet sky
Love flowing
Through my veins
As the
Midnight bells chime

There are stars
On my walls
Glow-in-the-dark dreams
Dreams of you and me
Two young lovers
Just drifting through
Space and time
Trying to find
Our way

Like the stars
On my walls
I want to shine
In your life

So
Every night
I wish on
These plastic stars

Starlight, starbright
The first star
I see tonight
I wish you
Were all mine

Oh Girl
There are mysteries
In the universe
Things
I can't explain

Like
How come
We can't connect
Shining bright
In each other's lives

There are stars
On my walls
Heaven above
In the velvet sky
Love flowing
Through my veins
As the
Midnight bells chime

Wishing
You were here
Lying by my side
Shining bright
In
Each other's lives
Like the
Stars on my walls.

**February 3, 2003**
**18 years old**

Joe Tallarigo

# Heaven Has A Plan

I
Don't know
What I see in you
We have
Nothing in common

Yet

When
I
Feel your touch
Gaze into your eyes
I see a plan
I don't understand

Heaven
Knows how it'll go
Fate
Brought us together
Both of us
Believing
God will
See us
Through the hard times
Bless us
Through the good times

Oh Girl
I'm beginning
To understand
Heaven
Has a plan
For
You and me

Staring at the night sky
I see a map of the universe
Some stars are crossed
Some stars are cursed
Some stars burn out
Some stars explode

Oh, Girl, I hope
We're the lucky ones
Who can make love last
Though I have
Fears and doubts
About how far
We can go

Heaven
Knows how it'll go
Fate
Brought us together
Both of us
Believing
God will
See us
Through the hard times
Bless us
Through the good times

Oh Girl
I'm beginning
To understand
Heaven
Has a plan
For
You and me.

**May 3, 2002**
**17 years old**

Joe Tallarigo

# Blowing Kisses To The Moon

I'm
Blowing kisses
To the moon
Hoping
You're looking up
Thinking about
Me and you

How one day
Though so far away
You'll be my bride
I'll be your groom

So Tonight
Instead
Of making wishes
I'm
Blowing kisses
To the moon

I'm
Blowing kisses
To the moon
Wanting to be
With you

But
All I have is
A picture of us
From our first date
I hold close
To my heart
Being apart
Is hard to do

So tonight
I'm
Blowing kisses
To the moon

I'm
Blowing kisses
To the moon

Hoping
A shooting star
Catches it
Delivers it
Straight to you
On the
Midnight Express

I want to
Rearrange the stars
To read
I love and miss you

But
I'm only
Blowing kisses
To the moon.

**\*\*January 22, 2006\*\***
**\*\*21 years old\*\***

Joe Tallarigo

# Have You Ever

Have you ever
Walked into a
Field of wildflowers
Felt love
Right then and there
With the one
You're holding hands with

Have you ever
Stolen a kiss
Underneath a full moon
Feeling butterflies
Flutter in your heart

Have you ever
Played in the rain
As everyone looked on
Cuddled in bed
As thunder roared

Have you ever
Though of their love
As snow
So pure and gentle
Easy to hold

I want to know
Have you ever
Been so in love
It makes you
Count the minutes
'Til
You're with them
For all your life

Have you ever
Danced all night long
That your feet
Ached for weeks

Have you ever
Thought about
The day
You'll be
Together forever
Waking up to
A world of two
Instead of one

Have you ever
Laid in a bed of roses
Feeling pure bliss
A love so true
It makes you cry

Have you ever

Because
I know I have

I have with you.

**June 2, 2008**
**23 years old**

Joe Tallarigo

# Kentucky Blue

No sweeter words were spoken
When she said
You were the best thing
That ever happened to me
When we met in the
Blue fields of Kentucky

Our
Summers were spent
Lying under the Falmouth sky
Counting stars and making wishes

Red
Is the color of love
But for me and you
It's Kentucky Blue

No sweeter words were spoken
When she said
You were the best thing
That ever happened to me
When we met in the
Blue fields of Kentucky

Soon
We were only a memory
Blowing through the trees
In the
Blue fields of Kentucky.

**May 31, 2005**
**20 years old**

# Chapter Six

# Country Road Philosophies

Joe Tallarigo

# One Good Song

There are times
I can't find the words
To finish a line
My creative mind
Freezes and crashes
Can't continue on
Everything is wrong
I feel like
A huge failure
In my
Creative endeavors

Then
Out of the blue
I listen to
One good song
The dam bursts open
The words start flowing
Sparking a
Creative fire in my soul
I'm right back
On top of the world

There are times
I get in ruts
Want to gut
Everything
I've written
Feel like
They're
Not up to par
Uninspiring
Want to walk away
From it all

Then
Out of the blue
I listen to
One good song
The dam bursts open
The words start flowing
Sparking a
Creative fire in my soul
I'm right back
On top of the world

One good song
Makes me grab
Pencil and paper
I jot down words
Then
Turn on my
Creative mind
To form
A good story
That I hope
Touches one soul

One good song
Can inspire
A whole book
When the words
Hit you deep
In your soul.

**August 20, 2020**
**35 years**

Joe Tallarigo

# Country Back Roads

It's funny
I love my home
Full of my favorite
Books, pictures, collectibles
Watching TV
Playing video games
I proclaim
My home
Is my comfort
Where everything
Has its place

Then
I get on these
Country back roads
All the comforts of home
Don't mean much anymore
Finding I could
Spend my whole life
Driving every
Country back road
Letting go of this world

Never-ending fields
Lonesome barns
Wide-open sky
Creeks that flow
One-lane roads
You don't feel
Closed-in
Never suffocating
On
Wall-to-wall people
Who are in a rush

These country roads
Makes me forget
All my comforts of home
I could spend my whole life
Driving every
Country back road
Letting go of this world

These
Country back roads
Don't need to know your name
Don't care what car you drive
Don't want you to rush
They need to be taken slowly
Enjoying every fence line
Pointing out every
Cow and horse
Out here
Time doesn't feel
Like a curse

Give me
Country back roads
Living free
Checking in on family
When I'm in town
Then It's
See you later
I don't want to be
Tied down
To a house
My restless soul
Craves the
Country back roads.

**\*\*January 11, 2026\*\***
**\*\*41 years old\*\***

Joe Tallarigo

# If I Live To Be 77

If I
Live to be
Seventy-seven
I'll thank
My lucky stars
Under Heaven

Tomorrow
Is never guaranteed

We need to
Stop and smell
The roses
Dance in the rain
Say hello
To our neighbors
Praise God
Everyday

If I
Live to be
Seventy-seven
I'll thank
My lucky stars
Under Heaven

It's time
For all negativity
To leave my soul
Start looking
For the good in people
Start eating better
Getting to bed earlier

It's time
To take chances
Free fall
Fly amongst the eagles
Touch the stars
Land on the moon

If I
Live to be
Seventy-seven
I'll thank
My lucky stars
Under Heaven

It's time
To play the
Piano and guitar
Sing a song
From my heart

Seventy-seven
I'm coming for you

But
I still have
A long way to go
Which
I'm going to enjoy
Every minute
Along the way.

**\*\*April 9, 2013\*\***
**\*\*28 years old\*\***

**(This is the 77<sup>th</sup> poem in the book)**

Joe Tallarigo

# Creativity
## (Part One)

I grew up
Watching
Movies and cartoons
That entertained me
Never thought much about
All the
Creativity and long hours
It takes
To develop each scene
Or know who the
Voice actors were

It wasn't until
I started attending
Comic cons in 2018
At the age of
Thirty-three
I had a revelation

Arts in school
Need to expand
Their courses
Let students create
Their own storyboards
Developing characters
Who go on journeys
Save the world

Let the students
Voice the characters
Learn proper technique
To take care of their voices
Take their ideas from
Paper to big screen

Who knows
Where I would be
If someone taught me
How animation was made
Instead of drawing still life's

Maybe
I would be
Voicing characters
Working alongside
The same voice actors
Who voiced
My favorite characters

Now
I'm forty-one
With a lot of
Pent-up
Creativity

Maybe one day
I'll make the leap
Pursue
Voice acting
Make my own cartoons
Cause I really love
Telling stories
Through my songs

How fun it would be
Signing photos
Of my characters
At comic-cons.

**\*\*January 12, 2026\*\***
**\*\*41 years old\*\***

Joe Tallarigo

# Creativity
## (Part Two)

I've been writing
My songs now
For twenty-five years
Much has changed
From my younger days
Of watching
Country Music videos
Listening to CDS
Attending concerts
Visiting
Nashville, Tennessee

You no longer need
Nashville, big labels
To pursue your
Smoky neon dreams
Movie videos are obsolete
You can find every song
On streaming
My favorite artists
Hardly tour anymore

But
These changes
Never
Discourage me

I still need my
Listening ears
Being observant
To expand
My creative mind

I now
Talk to
Eighth-graders
About being an author
And I'll tell you
What I tell them

You need to write daily
Up to a half-hour
Even if you write
A line or two
It's
Better than nothing
Expand your creativity
Listen to and read
Different genres
Show off your work
To your
Teachers and friends
Build a foundation

And only you can write
The story in your heart

The smartest thing
I ever did in
High school
Was proclaim
I wanted to be a
Country Music songwriter
Now I'm selling my books
At dozens of vendor shows
It's a thrill
Sharing my works.

**\*\*January 12, 2026\*\***
**\*\*41 years old\*\***

Joe Tallarigo

# The Dash

I enjoy
Walking through graveyards
Especially those
From the
1800s

My eager curiosity
Makes me wonder
What kind of life
Did they live
What did they enjoy
Most about their life

Were they immigrants
Did they witness
Any historical events
Do they still have any
Living relatives
Who can tell their stories
Since their dash
Can't speak for them

Their dashes
Make me reflect
On those I know
Whose dashes
Are carved in stone
From
Young to old
I hope they smile
As I
Tell their stories
Filling in their dash
Keeping their legacy alive

Do you ever
Stop and wonder
What your dash will be

Are you
Leaving behind a legacy
That people will remember
Who will
Proudly tell your stories
Of the good ol' days
Or are you
Leaving behind one
That will fade over time

A carved dash
Carved in stone
Representing
Our short time
Here on earth

So
When you
Come upon a graveyard
Pay your respects
For those whose homes
Are marble tombs
For they
Were once alive
Like you and me
And
Have to stories to tell.

**\*\*July 17, 2018\*\***
**\*\*33 years old\*\***

Joe Tallarigo

# Unlove The World

I'm going to
Unlove the world
Quit viewing it
From my carnal eye
Quit chasing expectations
Going to humble myself
Confess all my sins
Seeks forgiveness
Give up my worldly weight
Start heading down
The road less travelled

I'm going to
Supply the
Soul food and inspiration
For those
Chasing their dreams
Keep them on the
Straight and narrow
Protect them from
Satan's arrows
So they can fly
Amongst the angels

I've watched
Fortune and fame
Come and go
Saw the wind
Decide
What blows away
Learned real peace
Don't
Make a sound

I'm going to
Unlove the world
Don't want
Fame, glory, or gold
I want to be a leader
Teach people the truth
That god
Does love you
As his child
He's always around
Even in the
Darkest hours

I'm
Going to spend
My nights
Out in the desert
Admire
His wonders
In the velvet sky
Embracing
His presence
Let go of
This worldly weight
That holds me down

The truth and final reward
Is all I want
Out of this life.

**\*\*April 7, 2019\*\***
**\*\*34 years old\*\***

Joe Tallarigo

# Live Your Life

Take a stand
Of who you are
Be a nobody
Be a big star
Ride a horse
Drive a fast car
Sing your heart out
At every karaoke bar
Be the peace
Be the class clown

Live your life
We get many trips
Around the sun
But only get
One last breath
Make each
Moment count

No need to follow
The crowded paths
Carve your own way
Have your own say
Make your own rules
You're no longer
In school

Live your life
We get many trips
Around the sun
But only get
One last breath
Make each
Moment count

Stand up
For what you believe in
Be a leader
Be an outlaw

Sleep out in the desert
Beneath the stars
Take no
Map or compass
On your journeys
Let your heart
Be your guide

Live your life
We get many trips
Around the sun
But only get
One last breath
Make each
Moment count.

Go against the tide
Bend the lines
Set your sights
On the grand prize
Give more than
You take.

**\*\*March 2, 2005\*\***
**\*\*20 years old\*\***

Joe Tallarigo

# Let It Be Easy

You can't
Hold the wind
Or
Slow the sun
can't outrun time
once it begins

I've seen
The rich
Feel poor inside
Free men
Smiling
With nothing to hide

Let it be easy
Let it be true
I having
Nothing left to prove
Don't need answers
Carved in stone
Just a warm bed
I can call home

I've
Loved too hard
I've
Let love go
Both taught me
You can't
Make a heart
Stay tied down
Like you can't stop
Rain falling from
Town to town

Let it be easy
Let it be true
I having
Nothing left to prove
Don't need answers
Carved in stone
Just a warm bed
I can call home

If
Tomorrow comes
I'll take its hand
If It doesn't
I did
The best I could

Understand
There's no
Rhyme or reason
When
God decides
To call us home
We live a full life
Yet
We die alone

Let it be easy
Let it be true
I having
Nothing left to prove
Don't need answers
Carved in stone
Just a warm bed
I can call home.

**\*\*January 13, 2026\*\***
**\*\*41 years old\*\***

Joe Tallarigo

# I'm On The Rise

A ticking clock
A countdown drum
A steady beat
No one can outrun
Once time is up
There's no chance
For another dance

Storms may throw me
To the ground
Yet, I still stand

Streetlights blur
As I cross every line
Every doubt erased
When I see my name
On top of the page
Never needing luck
Never needing permission
I was built for this
Kind of collision

When the world says "Stop."
I say, "Watch me go."
Every mile feeding the flame
I'm on the rise
I'm ALIVE tonight
Heart on fire
Burning through the night

This is my moment
This is my time
I'm on the rise
Hear my name

Crashing through
Tearing down
Building up
My fighting spirit
A spark in the night
A guiding light

Every "no"
Puts lightning
In my veins
Every Fall
Taught me
How to sustain

When the world says "Stop."
I say, "Watch me go."
Every mile feeding the flame
I'm on the rise
I'm ALIVE tonight
Heart on fire
Burning through the night

I'm on the rise, can't stop me
Hear the thunder, feel its power
This is my moment, my sign
I'm on the rise, victory is mine

I didn't get this far
To turn around
Didn't fight this hard
To hit the ground
If destiny's calling
I'm answering loudly.

**January 13th, 2026**
**41 years old**

Joe Tallarigo

# That's Heaven
## (Part One)

Grandpa in his chair
Watching the Chicago Cubs
Drinking his beer
Imitating Harry Caray
Talking about his
Favorite Cubs Players
That's Heaven

Spending
Sunday afternoons
Playing Bingo
With my mom
Our friend Barb
Laughing and talking
Hoping we all win
That's Heaven

Going out to eat
With my aunt's
Telling them about
My school days
Talking about
Cincinnati sports
That's Heaven

Feeling the wind
On our faces
Running around
All day in the sun
Laughing
Carrying on
Eating penny candy
Swinging on swings
That's Heaven

Riding rollercoasters
Ramming cars
Walking to the
Cowboy town
Winning prizes
At the arcade
That's Heaven

Spending
 Days in Gatlinburg
Shopping
At every store
Eating a
Hot fudge sundae
At my favorite
Ice cream shop
That's Heaven

Trading and collecting
Sports cards and Pogs
Playing video games
Watching
Fox Kids, Kids WB,
Nickelodeon, Cartoon Network
That's Heaven

If Heaven
Is  anything close
To my childhood
Give me my wings
I'll fly away.

**January 17, 2026**
**41 years old**

Joe Tallarigo

# That's Heaven
## (Part Two)

Walking the hallways
Taking classes together
Rooting for our classmates
During every sports game
Slow dancing with your date
At every school dance
That's Heaven

Seeing my
Favorite singers live
Taking the music in
Singing along
Taking pictures
Getting an autograph
That's Heaven

Hanging out
With my brother
Our friends
In
Bowling Green, Ohio
Playing pool
Playing Halo
Box city
Ben Franklin's
That's Heaven

Writing and selling
My poetry books
Talking about writing
With other writers
Performing at open mics
That's Heaven

Spending my time with
My nieces and nephews
Sharing my childhood
Playing their favorite games
Watching their favorite shows
Going to the zoo
Playing putt-putt
That's Heaven

Planning and organizing
The Price Hill Thanksgiving Day Parade
With my friends
Seeing all the happy faces
Watching and walking in
The parade
Hosting the after-party
At Saint Lawrence
That's Heaven

If Heaven
Is  anything close
To my adulthood
Give me my wings
I'll fly away

Heaven is
Friendships, memories
The good times
Feeling alive
Doing what you love
Bringing joy to others
Carrying on traditions
That's my Heaven.

**\*\*January 23, 2026\*\***
**\*\*41 years old\*\***

# Chapter Seven

# The American Dream

# The American Dream

The American Dream
Doesn't belong to
The left or the right
Nor does it belong to
The day or the night
The rich or the poor
Nor is it exclusive
To the suits in DC

The American Dream
Can be rough
Can be turbulent
Can be rosy
Can be sweet
Can be under attack
Can be a shining light

The American Dream
Is what you see
What you want to achieve
Lots of perspiration
Lots of dedication
Lots of inspiration
Lots of conversation

Never giving up
Even when
The times get tough

Yes, it's true
I still believe in
The red, white, and blue

Joe Tallarigo

The American Dream
Is still the pulse
Of this Country
Coming together
To make it
Stronger and brighter
For all those
Who still believes

The American Dream
Is an unseen spirit
Firing up everyone
Who still

Wave the flag
Lends a helping hand
Stand up for those
Who can't
Those who
Work the land
Stand up and serve

I
Still believe in
The American Dream
while
The red, white, and blue
Still resonates
Through my veins.

**January 24, 2026**
**41 years old**

# 1990s Weather Channel

The
Hypnotic, relaxing
Jazz music
Playing during the
Local on the 8's
On the
1990s Weather Channel
Was magical
And instrumental
To us, 1990s kids
Introducing us to
Jazz and the weather

It was exciting
As a kid
Hearing my city
Being highlighted
During the forecasts

Be it
Rain, thunderstorms,
Warm, cold,
Ice, snow,
Floods, tornadoes

Those were
The good ol' days
Of my youth
Recording the
1990s Weather Channel
All day and night
On VHS tapes

Joe Tallarigo

I
Learned so much
About the weather
Watching the
1990s Weather Channel
Than
I did in
My science classes

Their live reports
From the cities
Being affected
By severe storms
Or heavy snow
Inspired me to
Go outside
During every storm
To feel the power of
Mother Nature

Those were
The good ol' days
Of my youth
Recording the
1990s Weather Channel
All day and night
On VHS tapes

Now these days
I record
The Weather Channel
And every storm
On my phone.

**January 24, 2026**
**41 years old**

# I Don't Want To Go Home

I
Don't want to go home
And go straight to bed
The music is still rattling
Around my head
My skin is still tingling
My heart is still racing
This natural high
Has me soaring

I need to shake loose
This good-time feeling
Let it all flow out
Need a place to unwind

I
Don't feel like eating
If I drive to the country
The moon and the stars
Will be my only company
What I'm really looking for
Is a party crowd
To burn off all this
Pent-up energy

God, lead me
To a neon sign
So I can continue
To have a good time
Listening to a jukebox
Dance with women
Have a few drinks
So
I can unwind

Joe Tallarigo

I
Don't want to go home
And go straight to bed
The music is still rattling
Around my head
My skin is still tingling
My heart is still racing
This natural high
Has me soaring

I need to shake loose
This good-time feeling
Let it all flow out
Need a place to unwind

It's only midnight
The party is
Only beginning

This good-time feeling
Will eventually pass
I'll crash hard
Like a young kid
On a sugar rush
You won't see me
For a few days
Need to
Sleep and recover
From being
On top of the world
Thanks to
The best concert
I've ever attended.

**June 24, 2018**
**33 years old**

# My Baseball Hall Of Fame

The
National Baseball Hall of Fame
In Cooperstown
Is the end all
For legendary careers
75% or higher votes
Punches your card
Into those hallowed halls
With a plaque
Hanging on the walls
For every fan to see

That's all
Fine and dandy
But growing up
We all had our
Favorite players
Who we believed
Would go all the way
Have their names called

Our favorite players
Who impacted the game
Made us want to play
All day in the sun
Buying their cards
Saving them in binders
Wore their jerseys
Played them in video games
Their banners and posters
Hanging on our walls
Watching them
At the stadium
Or on TV

Joe Tallarigo

Eric Davis, Mark Grace,
Dwight Gooden, Darryl Strawberry,
Jose Canseco, Don Mattingly,
Barry Bonds, Roger Clemens,
Sammy Sosa, Mark McGwire,
Chris Sabo, Sean Casey,
Will Clark, Andy Van Slyke,
Orel Hershiser, Kirk Gibson,
Dave Justice, Curt Schilling,
Greg Vaughn, Manny Ramirez,
John Franco, Jim Edmonds,
Lance Berkman, Keith Hernandez
Andrés Galarraga, Rafael Palmerio,
Jody Davis, Hideo Nomo

Those are
My favorite players
Who aren't in Cooperstown
But they are
In my
Baseball Hall of Fame

The ones
Who made me a
Fan, collector,
Played baseball
Attending games
To see them play
Who I have
On my teams
in video games.

**January 25, 2026**
**41 years old**

198

# Those Were The Days

Be caller ten
To win tickets
To next month's concert
Get registered
For backstage passes
Was my favorite
Radio contest

Dialing and redialing
As fast as I could
Saying a silent prayer
My call would go through
Let out a scream
When
I heard the DJ say
"What's your name
You just won
Two tickets
To next month's concert,"

Those were the days
Being a young teen
Winning concert tickets
To my favorite singers
Sometimes winning
A few times a year

You could say
I had
A magic touch
A lot of luck
Getting through
Being
Caller number ten

Joe Tallarigo

Every night
My Brother and I
Listened to Deliah
With the
Loving dedications
Sappy love songs
While we were
Destroying the world
Playing
Twisted Metal Two

Those were the days
Being a young teen
Learning
What love could be
Listening to all those
Sappy love songs
Spending time with
My younger Brother
Spending hours
Destroying the world

Those were the days
The late 1990s
The early 2000s
When
Radio was king
Listening to all
My favorite songs
Winning concert tickets
Learning
What love could be.

**January 26, 2026**
**41 years old**

# My Writing Philosophy

I don't put
Pencil to paper
Using my creativity
Writing out words
To submit them
To a panel of judges
To win awards
To gain recognition
That's not my style

You
Won't see me
Writing flowery poetry
Using fancy words
Writing for a cause
Writing for other poets
The ones who
Write for the
Gatekeepers and elitists

Nah,
My writing philosophy
My writing style
Is writing for
The common American
Who can also say
I've been there
Inspiring them
To write their stories
Like I have
Inspired by my
Country Music Hero
Merle Haggard

Joe Tallarigo

My publishing style
Is inspired by my other
Country Music Hero
Waylon Jennings
Breaking down doors
Expanding creativity
Doing things
Other poets
Have never done

I formed my own
Publishing company
Taking control
Of every step
Writing
One-hundred poems
Adding personal pictures
To enhance my books

You
Won't find me
Reading other poets
You'll find me
Listening to every
Music genre
To find inspiration
Using life events
To write my words

My greatest reward
Better than any award
Is having people tell me
They enjoyed my words.

**January 26, 2026**
**41 years old**

# Neon Dust

I
Wear my boots
On subway floors
Steel tracks hum
Like an old back porch
Have a hat full of miles
A pocket full of dreams
Trading open skies
For silver screens

Streetlights flicker
Like campfire flames
Strangers are strangers
Never exchanging names

Still
I tip my brim
To the moon up high
Same one hanging
Over a prairie sky

I'm a neon cowboy
In a city of chrome
Concrete trails
I'm riding alone
Chasing a song
Only I can hear
Been here a year
With no luck
Still I walk
Tall, wild, and free
Kicking up hope
In neon dust

Joe Tallarigo

I walk by
Coffee shops
Where the poets
Hide and write
Every open mic
A chance to rise
To the big time
Though flaming out
Costs a piece of pride

I'm a neon cowboy
In a city of chrome
Concrete trails
I'm riding alone
Chasing a song
Only I can hear
Been here a year
With no luck
Still I walk
Tall, wild, and free
Kicking up hope
In neon dust

Mama said
"Son,
Don't trade your name
For a flicker
of borrowed flame,"

So, I hold on tight
Like reins in the middle
Of a rodeo.

**January 27, 2026**
**41 years old**

204

# His Last Ride

He laces up his boots
Puts on his lucky
Belt and cowboy hat
A tear in his eyes
Lightning in his veins
He knows what's at stake

Twenty years
Competing in
The rodeo circuit
Winning gold buckles
A few broken bones
Now he's preparing
For his final
Eight-second ride

He enters the chute
Climbs on the back
On the bull
They call Midnight
The announcers announce
This is his last ride
The crowd cheers
Continuing
As the chute opens

He holds on with one hand
Gripping tight on the strap
Midnight snorts and bucks
He grips tighter
Determined
To give this crowd
What they came for
Want to go out on top

Joe Tallarigo

The horn blows
He's done it
Eight-seconds
The judges give him
A ninety-four
The crowd goes wild
As he exits
His heart pounding
His soul somber
His last ride
Is now done

He watches
The crowd leave
Takes a deep breath
Reflecting on the last
Twenty years
Feeling natural highs
Getting stomped on
Getting thrown
Into the sky
Always determined
To get an
Eight-second ride

He
Made his mark
In the
Professional Rodeo
Cowboy Association
As a
Tough rodeo man
A yearly champion.

**April 30, 2019**
**34 years old**

# Happy 250<sup>th</sup> Birthday, America

Grab your boots
Tailgates open wide
Smoking ribs and briskets
Slide on inside
This party is
Going to be rocking

America is turning
Two hundred fifty
Time to celebrate
Our national pride

Red, white, and blue
All over the place
This is America
Freedom and fireworks
Sparkling
In the Summer nights
Eagles still flying high
Jamming in the country
Living the moment
That's the recipe

Hey neighbor
Welcome
Join us
Grab yourself
A full plate
Eat amongst
Friends and neighbors
Let's be
United

Joe Tallarigo

Kids are running
Wild
That's their
Fun
Ours begins when
The sun goes
Down
You'll hear us
Two towns
Over

Red, white, and blue
All over the place
This is America
Freedom and fireworks
Booming
On this
Fourth of July
Eagles flying high
Jamming in the country
Living the moment
That's the recipe

Flags waving
Pride pulsating
USA chanting

America
Happy 250th, Birthday
Going to celebrate
You
All year long.

**January 27, 2026**
**41 years old**

# Stars and Pine Cones
## (Part 2)

These
Past fourteen years
Have been
A blessing
Watching
You grow up
From your
Stars and pine cone days

Getting to give you
Various experiences
Lifelong memories
We sure
Had a lot of fun

Watching
Disney movies
Playing
Disney Princess games
On my IPOD

Attending
Cincinnati Reds games
Taking
You and your brother
To meet
Cincinnati Reds players

Spending afternoons
At
The Cincinnati Zoo
Loveland Castle
Krohn Conservatory
Delhi Park

Joe Tallarigo

It's a thrill
Seeing your face
Light up
Meeting
Your favorite
Voice actors
At different
Comic-cons

Now
Time is
Flying by
You're now
Eighteen and graduating
Chasing
Your dream job
Time for you
To fly
Find your place
In this world

You sure
Have come a long way
From your
Stars and pine cones days

I'm
Proud of you
My little friend!

**January 28, 2026**
**41 years old**

# Stars and Pine Cones
## (Part 2)

Joe Tallarigo

# Ode To The Duke Boys

Red and blue lights
Flashing behind me
It's not even
Five o'clock
Driving on these
Country back roads
Admiring the scenery
Wondering
What I did wrong

I put the
Pedal to the metal
Channeling my
Inner Duke boys
Johnny Law
Isn't going
To catch me

Just wish
I had a
General Lee
To go flying
Through the air
Yelling
"Yee-Haw"
As my life
Flashes
Before my eyes
Landing
On the other side

Leaving
Jonny Law
In the dust

There's nothing
But a long
One-lane dirt road
With rows of corn
Johhny Law
Is honking their horn
Wanting me to stop
But I've got to top
The Duke Boys
They would find a way
To make their escape
Live for another day

I'm
Channeling my
Inner Duke boys
Johnny Law
Is on my tail
Either they want
To give me a ticket
Or
Haul my behind
To the county jail

How I wish
I had Daisy
By my side
To make this
Police chase
Even more
Fun and adventurous
Escaping
Johnny Law.

**\*\*January 31, 2026\*\***
**\*\*41 years old\*\***

Joe Tallarigo

# 1990S Country
## (Part One)

Tim McGraw
Was "Everywhere"
Joe Diffie
Was a "Pick-up Man"
Geroge Strait
Said "Write This Down"
Kenny Chesney
Wanted to know
"How Forever Feels"

Martina McBride
Was a "Happy Girl"
LeAnn Rimes
Was "Blue"
Shania Twain
Said "Come On Over"
Deanna Carter
Made us crave
"Strawberry Wine"

George Jones
Had "Choices"
Montgomery Gentry
Put on their "Hillbilly Shoes"
Brad Paisley
Asked "Who Needs Pictures"
Little Texas
Made us think
"What Might Have Been"

Oh 1990s Country
Where did you go
Can we go back
To these times

LeAnn Womack
Was "The Fool"
The Dixie Chicks
Were "Ready to Run"
Trisha Yearwood
Asked "How Do I Live"
SheDaisy were
Saying their
"Little Goodbyes"

Kenny Rogers
Was "The Greatest"
Garth Brooks
Was "Calling Baton Rouge"
Alan Jackson
Proclaimed "I'll Try"
Tracy Lawrence
Gave us advice
"Time Marches On"

Patty Loveless
Was "High On Love"
Faith Hill
Was a "Wild One"
Jo Dee Messina
Proclaimed "I'm Alright"
Reba McEntire
Gave us the advice
"The Heart Won't Lie"

Oh 1990s Country
Where did you go
Can we go back
To these times?

**January 29, 2026**
**41 years old**

# 1990S Country
## (Part 2)

Tracy Byrd
Did "The Watermelon Crawl"
Sawyer Brown
"Took the Dirt Road"
Diamond Rio
Wanted "To Meet In The Middle"
Alabama
Said
"Forever is as far as I'll Go"

Mary Chapin Carpenter
Was partying
"Down At The Twist And Shout"
Reba McEntire
Was "Falling Out Of Love"
Pam Tillis
Said
"Don't Tell Me What To Do"
Faith Hill
Said to her man
"Let's Go To Vegas"

Alan Jackson
"Chased A Neon Rainbow"
Brooks and Dunn
Did some
"Boot Scooting Boogie"
Billy Ray Cyrus
Didn't want a
"Achy Breaky Heart"

1990s Country Music
I miss you so
Can we go back

Wynonna Judd
"Saw The Light"
Martina McBride
Had "Wild Angels"
LeAnn Rimes
Had a
"One-Way Ticket"

David Ball
Had a "Thinking Problem"
Clint Black
Had
"A Good Run Of Bad Luck"
David Lee Murphy
Was looking for
"A Party Crowd"
Toby Keith
Asked his former flame
"How Do You Like Me Now"

Shania Twain
Said
"Honey, I'm Home"
The Dixie Chicks
Needed
"Wide Open Spaces"
Lila McCann
Said
"I Wanna Fall In Love"

1990s Country Music
I miss you so
Can we go back?

**January 30, 2026**
**41 Years Old**

Joe Tallarigo

# Circle Of Light

One hundred years
Of
Stories and hard times
From the
Louisiana Bayous
The Great Plains
Big 'ol cities
The Smoky Mountains
All come together
To entertain us
From a wooden circle
Every Saturday Night

Dreamers, comedians,
Fiddlers, banjo pickers,
Outlaws, traditionalists,
The new stars
The rhinestoners
All come together
To play their songs
Standing
In the shadows
Of those giants
Who came before

The circle of light
Has always shone
Where the
Bluegrass rings
Fiddles play tight
From Roy Acuff
To brand new stars
It's the Opry
No matter where you are

Do you know
It's still the
Beating heart of
Country Music
Many youngsters
Want to take their guitars
To blow off the roof
With fancy grooves
Memorable hooks
On every
Saturday night

If you ever hear
Hank Williams
Moan the blues
Minnie Pearl
Yell "How-Dee"
Witness
Johnny Cash
Kick out the footlights
You're now officially
Part of the Opry family

The circle of light
Has always shone
Where the
Bluegrass rings
Fiddles play tight
From Roy Acuff
To brand new stars
It's the Opry
No matter where you are.

**January 30, 2026**
**41 years old**

(This is the 100<sup>th</sup> poem in the book)

Joe Tallarigo